'You're afraid your next-door neighbour will get too familiar.'

In point of fact he was wrong. It was herself she was afraid of. 'Not at all...'

'Sarah, will you just take down my phone number? If you want me, I can be over there in seconds.'

Sarah stiffened at the hint of command in his tone, but quickly scribbled the name he gave her on a notepad. 'There. I've got it, but you won't be disturbed, I promise... Alex,' she added with sudden contrition, 'thank you. It's very thoughtful of you.'

'I told you I was a secret romantic,' he said. 'If you're in distress at any time I absolutely insist on charging to your rescue.'

Catherine George was born in Wales, and early developed a passion for reading which eventually fuelled her compulsion to write. Marriage to an engineer led to nine years in Brazil, but on his later travels the education of her son and daughter kept her in the UK. And instead of constant reading to pass her lonely evenings she began to write the first of her romantic novels. When not writing and reading she loves to cook, listen to opera, browse in antique shops and walk the Labrador.

Recent titles by the same author:

EARTHBOUND ANGEL
THE RIGHT CHOICE
NO MORE SECRETS

LIVING NEXT DOOR TO ALEX

BY
CATHERINE GEORGE

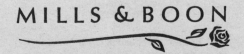

MILLS & BOON

*All the characters in this book have no existence outside the imagination
of the author, and have no relation whatsoever to anyone bearing the
same name or names. They are not even distantly inspired by any
individual known or unknown to the author, and all the incidents are
pure invention.*

*First published in Great Britain 1996
Harlequin Mills & Boon Limited,
Eton House, 18-24 Paradise Road, Richmond, Surrey TW9 1SR*

© Catherine George 1996

ISBN 0 263 79956 5

*Set in Times Roman 10 on 12 pt.
02-9702-54053 C1*

*Printed and bound in Great Britain
by Mackays of Chatham PLC, Chatham*

CHAPTER ONE

A BRAHMS sonata for piano and cello, played with great verve and passion, filled the Great Hall of Ingham Lacey with exquisite sound, and Sarah, from her perch on a stool tucked behind a suit of armour, listened with pleasure to the two talented young performers. But, magical though it was, this type of evening was no novelty to her. As always her eyes strayed to the tapestry over the great door, which showed Alexander the Great extending mercy to the family of Darius, defeated King of the Persians. The tapestry's fragility and age made it difficult for a stranger to identify the subject without the help of the guidebook, but Sarah, long familiar with the skill of the medieval weavers, could see the overt interest in the conqueror's attitude as he surveyed the women at his mercy. She gazed at Alexander indulgently, then turned her head a fraction, some sixth sense telling her she was being watched. From across the hall eyes held hers for a moment, bright beneath dark brows in a face just visible through the rows of rapt music-lovers.

Sarah smiled politely and turned away, pleased with the turn-out for the charity concert. The hall was great only by definition, and a concert only paid dividends if all the seats were sold. The room's description came from the raftered roof which soared to almost forty feet above the floor. But this particular Great Hall, relatively small compared to those in other ancient houses, had always been the heart of the house, virtually unchanged since the Wars of the Roses, give or take a stained-glass window or two. And the acoustics were superb. Tonight, filled with people willing to pay generous prices for tickets, the Great Hall came into its own, vibrant with life and music.

The Allegro came to an end, and as the applause began for the smiling, bowing young women, Sarah slipped into the outer hall. As she'd expected, all the stewards were ready at their stations for the interval. Jugs of iced fruit juice, bottles of wine and mineral water, glasses, nuts and canapés were laid out on a seventeenth-century oak refectory table, ready to refresh the concertgoers on a hot evening more typical of midsummer than early May.

In the absence of the custodian, Colonel Newby, late of the Gordon Highlanders, Sarah stood alongside the warden to chat with concertgoers as they streamed from the Great Hall, and to press them towards the refreshments. After a while she left Jack Wells to the task and began shepherding those with drinks outside into the cobbled courtyard, to ease the crush inside. To her immense satisfaction a new moon hung in the darkening, gilt-edged sky.

'I'm impressed,' said a voice in Sarah's ear, and she turned to meet the eyes last seen smiling at her pre-occupation with the tapestry.

'With the music?'

'That too. The girls are brilliant musicians. But I meant the entire occasion. Good music, a lot of money channelled to a children's charity, the atmosphere of this incredible house—and even a moon to complete the picture. Value for money at twice the price!'

'We aim to please,' smiled Sarah, noting that the eyes surveyed her with rather flattering interest. They were set at a slant above a prominent nose in a swarthy face, below dark, close-curling hair. The nose, she noted, had been broken at some time, giving him a tough look all of a piece with his physique. The lightweight suit and conventional white shirt did little to disguise a build any heavyweight boxer would have coveted.

'You like Brahms?' he asked.

'Very much. Though I shall enjoy the Shostakovich fireworks later just as much.' She beckoned to one of the stewards, who was approaching with a tray. 'Do have another drink.'

'If you'll join me, I will, thank you.' Her companion accepted a glass of fruit juice in place of the wine he'd just finished. 'Driving,' he explained with a smile. 'Tell me, what's the subject of the tapestry you were studying? I couldn't make it out.'

Sarah cast an eye round the crowded courtyard to check that guests were being offered refills, and decided she could safely return her attention to her companion, who, surprisingly, appeared to be alone. 'It's Alexander the Great's visit to the family of the defeated Darius. If you look long enough you can see he's eyeing the women with quite blatant interest.'

The dark face lit with a glint of square white teeth as he grinned. 'I thought Alexander's interests lay in different directions.'

'The artist who worked the tapestry obviously kept an open mind.' Sarah smiled back, and finished her fruit juice. 'I must see if our young musicians need anything before the second half. If you'll excuse me? Enjoy the Shostakovich.'

Once everyone was back in place in the Great Hall, and the music had begun again, Sarah found her attention straying from the Shostakovich fireworks to thoughts of the attractive stranger. When the performance was over it was with some regret that she left Jack Wells and the stewards to speed the departing guests on their way. Instead, as usual, she went to oversee the supper laid on for the young musicians.

In her capacity as housekeeper at Ingham Lacey, knowing perfectly well that she looked surprisingly young for the post, Sarah kept firmly to a policy of impersonal friendliness with male visitors. And was rarely tempted to respond with anything warmer. But for once she'd been quite tempted to stay and chat, liking the easy friendliness of the tall, dark stranger. Like a fortune in the tea-leaves, she thought, laughing at herself as she plied the tired young performers with smoked salmon and strawberries. By the time they were ready to leave all the guests had gone, one striking male guest included.

Next morning there was the usual concerted effort by all hands to get the Great Hall cleared of seating and the grand piano removed in good time for the midday zero hour when the public was let in. Afterwards a swift, practised inspection of the public rooms reassured Sarah that Ingham Lacey was ready and waiting, everything in place, each steward in position, and the shop ready to supply the public with all the usual souvenirs.

She made time for a sandwich and a cup of coffee in the tea-room, then hurried across the velvet grass of the croquet lawn to the Elizabethan stable block. Her own quarters were at one end, and the gardener and his family lived at the other, flanking the two holiday cottages which had been refurbished and redecorated only a year previously. As always, the cleaning team had left the cottages immaculate. Sarah ran a practised eye over every detail, checking that everything was ready, wood floors gleaming, carpets swept, every piece of antique furniture glossy with beeswax.

She locked up, thinking it was a pity that the larger cottage, which could accommodate five people in comfort, or seven at a pinch, was to house one solitary man for two whole weeks of the holiday season. Not that it affected her administrative costs. The charges for the two holiday lets were per cottage, not per person. And this man was no ordinary holidaymaker. He represented the consortium which owned the entire property.

The medieval, moated house of Ingham Lacey had undergone many additions and modifications over the centuries since it was first erected in the fourteenth, but had managed to remain in private ownership until a mere ten years previously, when it passed into the hands of a group of businessmen. They employed a custodian, a warden, a head gardener and a housekeeper, several enthusiastic, well-informed people as stewards, and opened the historic building four days a week to the public.

Ingham Lacey owed its survival, and its restoration, to a young Scottish soldier, one Alec Mackenzie, who had come across the house while on leave in Kent in the Second World War. When the war was over he married his wartime sweetheart, a Kentish maid anxious to remain near her family. Armed only with grit, determination and the money to buy one solitary bus, Alec Mackenzie gradually built up a fleet of coaches into a nationwide transport company. But all the time he never abandoned his dream of Ingham Lacey.

His son, Alexander, cut from the same astute cloth, went on to expand the family business to include haulage and a small commercial airline. When the owner of Ingham Lacey finally died Alexander Mackenzie, on his father's instructions, bought the property on behalf of Mackenzie Holdings and hired conservators and restorers to preserve its fragile, ancient allure. Old Alec lived just long enough to see his dream come true. And now, thought Sarah with misgiving, his grandson, Alexander Mark 3, was here on a two-week visit.

Unlike the Alexander in the tapestry, Alex Mackenzie the Third's sexual preferences were channelled entirely towards the opposite sex, something Sarah had learned quite by chance from her sister. Jane's employer had an attractive daughter who'd been deeply involved for a time with Alex Mackenzie. Due to Sarah's connections with Mackenzie Holdings Jane had taken great interest in the affair, and reported when it was over, telling Sarah it had lasted longer than Alex Mackenzie's usual relationships, though the disappointed Camilla had fully expected a wedding ring, and needed a protracted luxury cruise in the sun to recover from the blow.

And now this same Alex Mackenzie was coming here to stay. Why? Wild rumours were rife among the staff. Sarah officially pooh-poohed them, but alone at night in her cottage she worried. So far she'd heard that Mackenzie Holdings had plans to close the house to the public, turn it into a hotel, develop it as a conference centre, even build a theme park in the five hundred acres of beautiful Kent farmland that surrounded it. Sarah shuddered, redid her face and hair, and gave depressed consideration to applications for another job as she stationed herself at her window to wait.

Sarah had been housekeeper at Ingham Lacey for nearly three years, and loved everything about her job, including her tiny cottage in the stable block, the home that went with the post. Until she knew what Mr Mackenzie had in mind she would make a point of radiating efficiency, along with a sugar-coating of sweetness and light if she felt the occasion, or Mr Mackenzie, demanded it. And it would help her keep her job. Which it might if he was as responsive to women as Jane said.

When a car came down the narrow lane and turned into the private parking space in the small field opposite the stable block Sarah left her cottage, conscious of a feeling of anticlimax when she found a young couple extracting a baby from the car.

'Mr and Mrs Henderson?' She smiled warmly. 'I'm Sarah Law, the housekeeper at Ingham Lacey. I hope you had a good journey?'

It took very little time for Sarah to admire the smiling baby girl, show the tired young couple over the smaller, two-storey cottage, hand over the keys and assure them that she or Jack Wells, the warden, were on hand to answer any queries. Back in her own cottage Sarah made coffee in her kitchen, and had finished it, along with half *The Times* crossword, before her doorbell rang, by which time she was feeling rather tense. Sarah braced herself and went to open the door, to find herself face to face with the man she'd met at the concert. This time he was dressed in jeans and an open-necked chambray shirt with rolled-up sleeves, and looked, if anything, even more attractive than he had in a formal suit.

'Why, hello!' His eyes lit up. 'This is a pleasant surprise. I'm looking for Miss Law, the housekeeper.'

'I'm Miss Law,' Sarah informed him, hoping her dismay wasn't showing. Was this...?

'My name's Mackenzie,' he announced. He held out his hand, his mouth downturned in a wry smile. 'Are you really the housekeeper? I expected someone older, with a black dress and a bunch of keys, like Mrs Danvers in *Rebecca*.'

'I do have a bunch of keys.' Sarah smiled politely to cover her disappointment. She'd been very much attracted to the man she'd thought was just another music-lover. To find that he was actually Alex Mackenzie was a definite turn-off. She took the keys from her desk and closed her door behind her. 'If you'll just come next door I'll show you round the cottage.'

She led the way along the brick path to the larger cottage, opened the door and motioned the new arrival down the step straight into the sitting-room. 'Please take care. The ceilings here, as you can see, are low. The entrance into the kitchen in particular is a hazard to taller visitors.'

He grinned ruefully as he stood in the middle of the room, his hair grazing the central beam.

'Has anyone suffered concussion yet?' he asked.

'Happily no—just the odd bruise so far.'

Alex Mackenzie looked round him in approval. The room was furnished with a pair of comfortable sofas covered in striped crimson fabric, with rose-printed linen at the leaded windows, a low table in the middle of the room, an old desk in one corner, and lamps placed at strategic points. 'I like it,' he said, and Sarah smiled, deciding not to mention that the decor was largely her own choice.

She led the way into the adjoining dining-room, which was furnished in a simple, functional style with a pine table and rush-seated chairs. Sarah indicated the step up into the kitchen. 'This is where taller guests take extra care. The kitchen is fully equipped, but not large, as you can see.'

When Alex Mackenzie joined her in it, ducking his head, the kitchen felt oppressively small. Swiftly Sarah opened cupboards, displayed the washing machine and demonstrated the workings of the combination microwave and cooker, then opened a tall cupboard to reveal a fire extinguisher.

'Smoking isn't possible in the cottage, of course. There's a smoke alarm in each room, and I must warn you that if the alarms go off in the house the warning will sound in here too. And vice versa,' she added.

He grinned. 'At which point I take to the hills?'

'Vacate the premises at the double, anyway,' she agreed. 'Don't worry. We practise fire-drills regularly. Now if you'll follow me upstairs, please.'

The stairs led straight from the sitting-room to a large landing with a fireplace, with an arrangement of dried flowers on the hearth. Sarah waved a hand at the small, functional bathroom and the single bedroom with ornamental wrought-iron bars at the window.

'A safety measure for younger guests.' She went on into the main bedroom, where the dominant feature was a king-sized bed with a half-tester hung with the same subtly printed fabric covering the chaise longue beneath one of the windows. A Jacobean settle stood at the foot of the bed, and in one corner a chest with a swivel mirror served as a dressing table. For a wardrobe there was an old oak armoire; a full-length pier glass stood near the door, and the deep window embrasures held ceramic jugs and ornaments. It was a romantic, charming room, and guests always exclaimed with pleasure at the sight of it. Alex Mackenzie said nothing.

Sarah waited a moment then led the way up to the top floor, pointing out that in the attic bedroom, in addition to the usual furniture, a chest held a rope ladder fire-escape.

'I hope you'll be comfortable, Mr Mackenzie,' she said, and went downstairs swiftly. 'If you need anything, I live next door, though during the day I'm mostly in the house. Jack Wells, the warden, is temporarily putting up in the custodian's apartments while Colonel Newby's away, but he's around all the time if you need him. The head gardener, Tim Sewell, lives with his wife, Janet, and their two children in the cottage at the far end of the stable block. He'll be happy to give you a guided tour of the grounds.'

By this time they were back in the sitting-room and Sarah felt restive in the unbroken silence from her companion. 'Any questions, Mr Mackenzie?'

'The gardens,' he said, looking through the window, 'and the house itself. Are there any restrictions?'

'Visitors to the holiday cottages are welcome in the house itself any time during the periods when it is open to the public, and in the gardens and the wilderness at any time up until nightfall, when the security lights and alarms come into operation.' Sarah looked at him levelly. 'Of course you aren't the usual holidaymaker, Mr Mackenzie, so the rules don't really apply to you. If you wish to visit the house when it's closed to the public, and inspect it alone, please approach me or Jack Wells for the keys and we'll leave you to it.'

'What if I make off with some of the valuables in there?' He nodded towards the sunlit stone pile.

'Since they belong to you—or to the consortium—it's not within my province to object if you do,' said Sarah, then softened the tartness of her retort with a smile. Sweetness and light, she reminded herself. 'Only if you do fancy anything, please let me know so I can alter my inventory.'

'I was joking,' he said wryly.

'Yes, of course.'

Their eyes met for a moment, then Sarah looked at her watch. 'I must get back to the house.'

He barred her way as she made to leave. 'Miss Law, wait a minute. I wondered if you could give me a list of places to eat round here—country pubs and so on.'

'Certainly.' Sarah crossed the room to the desk, pulling forward two leatherbound folders. 'This one tells you about Ingham Lacey, also about various other places of interest in the area. The other one has information about inns and restaurants and so on.'

'Can you recommend any of them personally?' he asked, leaning over her shoulder to look.

Sarah moved away, and went to the door. 'Jack Wells or the Sewells know more on the subject than me, Mr Mackenzie, though I can recommend the Roebuck in the village if you'll settle for good pub fare. Now if that's all I must get back to the house. It's almost time to close up for the day. Welcome to Ingham Lacey. I'll leave the keys here in the door. Enjoy your stay.'

'Thank you. I intend to.' He smiled, and, remembering her vow, Sarah gave him a smile of such warmth in return that his eyes narrowed.

'What's your first name?' he asked abruptly.

'Sarah.'

'I'm Alex.' He grinned. 'It saves confusion at home. My father's Alexander.'

Preferring not to admit that she knew all that, Sarah said goodbye, and went back to her own cottage and out through the kitchen door into her little private garden, securing the gate behind her before threading her way through the visitors lingering to enjoy the gardens.

It was late that evening before the usual security checks had been made and both Sarah and Jack Wells were satisfied that all was well with the house. As Sarah walked back to her quarters the hot day was giving way languorously to a scented twilight, and lamps were burning in every cottage in the stable block bar her own.

A sudden sharp pang of loneliness surprised her by its sheer novelty. Her work at the house was absorbing, and her quiet life in this remote, wooded Kent valley so much to her taste that, far from feeling lonely, Sarah rarely left it except for visits to her family. Her chaste retreat, Jane called it. Though, as Sarah never failed to point out, the so-called retreat was a mere thirty-minute drive from the M25 London orbital motorway. In miles, anyway. In all other ways it was another world, and loneliness something rare in her experience at Ingham Lacey.

Sarah shook off the unexpected mood, loaded her washing machine, then typed several answers to queries about the holiday cottages, which were fully booked for the current season. She expressed regrets, invited applications for the following season, then, in no mood to cook anything, put together a supper of cheese and salad and ate it at her kitchen table, with the daily paper propped in front of her. Pleased to read that the hot, dry spell of weather was expected to continue for the next few days, she decided to hang her washing out on the line in the field behind the cottage and leave it there overnight.

She hefted the laundry basket, picked up a torch and crossed the lane to the field, carefully picking her way past the tree where an old-fashioned wooden swing hung for younger visitors. She breathed in deeply, filling her lungs with blossom-scented air as she pegged out bed-linen and towels, watching the firefly glow of an airliner making a descent distant enough to be noiseless in the still, starry night.

How beautiful it was here, she thought with sudden passion, ignoring the memory of snow and frost, and days grey with rain and mist. She'd do her damnedest to stay here, and if it meant buttering up the rather fascinating Mr Mackenzie she would. If he did intend creating a conference centre, or even just a private retreat for his fellow businessmen to enjoy, he'd still need a housekeeper. And she was good at her job.

Sarah picked up her basket and the torch, the latter unnecessary now that her eyes were accustomed to the light. She strolled slowly down the hill, then halted as a tall shape detached itself from one of the trees.

'Don't be alarmed, Miss Law,' said Alex Mackenzie. 'I came out here to enjoy a cigar and this incredible night at the same time.'

'Good evening,' she said serenely. 'I was hanging out my laundry.'

'Don't you have a machine to deal with that?' he asked, surprised, and took the basket from her.

Butter, Sarah reminded herself, and let him. 'I do have a drier, but it uses a lot of electricity. In weather like this I save energy and money and make use of free fresh air. By the way,' she added, with a lilt of amusement in her voice, 'if you want to hang out your own laundry there's a clothes line for visitors just over there. Though the Hendersons have a young baby, so you may have to fight for space now and then.'

'Would I put myself outside your personal pale for ever if I said the idea of laundry never crossed my mind?' he asked wryly. 'I packed enough clothes to last my stay.'

Sarah laughed, and walked with him through the gate and across to the cottages. Alex accompanied her to her front door, and looked down into the face illumined by the light from her sitting-room.

'Can I ask you something?' he said, his tone utterly serious.

'Of course.'

'Your record is on file with us. But no personal details. I know you've been with us for three years and you live here alone. But the job seems a strange choice for a woman like you.'

Was he already assessing her suitability for her job? 'I'm not quite sure what you mean, Mr Mackenzie,' she said warily.

There was silence for a moment, then Alex handed her the basket. 'I mean, to be blunt, that you're young, clever and very good-looking. Yet you choose a job which virtually cuts you off from the real world in this place.'

'I was very lucky to get a job I love—and which I do very well,' she added deliberately.

'I know you do,' he assured her. 'The fact's self-evident from the way this place is run. We're lucky to have you.

I was just curious about any immediate plans which might necessitate a move on your part.'

'If you mean another job, no, I haven't. No other job could compare with this one as far as I'm concerned.'

He smiled. 'My attempt at tact obscured my meaning. I wondered if there was a man in your life, wanting to tempt you away from here.'

If he'd been anyone else Sarah would have given him short shrift, told him it was none of his business. But Alex Mackenzie was entitled to know, she reminded herself. 'No. No one,' she said briskly.

He frowned, lounging against the door lintel as he gazed down at her. 'You surprise me. As you know— because you caught me at it—I couldn't help looking at you when you were gazing at that tapestry last night; the profile and the bright hair against the grey stone of the wall caught my attention. Then I witnessed the sudden transformation as you supervised everything so efficiently in the interval. I didn't know exactly who you were then. But which one *is* you, Miss Law? The dreamer with the tapestry? Or the efficient housekeeper who runs a very tight ship at Ingham Lacey?'

'Very definitely the latter, Mr Mackenzie.' She smiled, her dark eyes dancing. 'When I was staring at that tapestry I was thinking what a hassle it is to clean it. Goodnight.'

CHAPTER TWO

INGHAM LACEY was closed to the public the next day. Sarah spent the morning with the cleaning team, doing a little hands-on work herself on some of the ceramics. She carried a wire tray lined with felt to the drawing-room, placed four Chelsea figurines in it, separated from each other by wads of bubble wrap, then carried the tray to the butler's pantry, where the light was best to deal with the delicate bocage—the leaves and flowers which so easily snapped off.

She was plying a hogshair brush with care, its metal ferrule swathed in insulation tape to protect the fragile piece, when Jack Wells came in.

Jack was a retired fire officer in his early fifties, large, unflappable and utterly dependable. He was responsible for security, and the overseeing of the builders who carried out restoration work on the property. He lived with his wife in the lodge at the entrance to Ingham Lacey, but in the absence of Colonel Newby he was temporarily sleeping alone in the latter's apartments.

'Sarah, Mr Mackenzie's asking if you can spare him some time today to show him over the house.'

She replaced the dusted figurine in its nest carefully and raised an eyebrow at him. 'Did he say when?'

Jack grinned. 'Any time convenient for you.' He paused, eyeing her as she began applying her brush to another flower-encrusted figurine. 'Seems a nice chap, Sarah.'

20

'Yes. He does. I just wish he wasn't Alex Mackenzie.'

'Alex?' queried Jack slyly.

'That's how he's known, apparently.'

'Has he said anything to you? About the plans for Ingham Lacey?'

'No. Perhaps he will this afternoon. Tell him two o'clock, Jack. I'll have done the drawing-room ceramics by lunchtime.' She straightened. 'Would you mind if we used Colonel Newby's sitting-room in the private apartments at some stage? Mr Mackenzie may be inclined to talk business after a tour of the house.'

Jack shrugged. 'Feel free. I won't be back in there until bedtime. Liz still won't come with me. Stubborn woman. Never known her fanciful about anything else, but she digs her heels in about a night in the house.'

'Afraid she'll run into Sir Edward Frome!'

'That's about the size of it.' Jack shrugged his burly shoulders. 'I've spent many a night there when the Newbys are away. Never met the ghost yet.'

Sarah laid another figurine in the basket. 'If you do, please introduce him to me—I'd love to meet him! Right, tell Mr Mackenzie I'll be here in the butler's pantry.'

Alex Mackenzie presented himself on the stroke of two, just as the stable clock chimed the hour.

Sarah looked up with a smile from the Derby vase she was cleaning. 'Good afternoon, Mr Mackenzie. Did you survive your first night in the cottage uninjured?'

He grinned. 'Just about. I'm developing a defensive stoop. By the end of the fortnight I'll look like Quasimodo.'

There was nothing hunched about him at the moment, thought Sarah appreciatively. He looked supremely fit, his face glowing as though he'd spent the morning in the sun. He wore a white polo shirt and chinos, with rubber-soled deck shoes on his bare brown feet.

Sarah had rather sheepishly taken time with her face after lunch, and changed into a clean yellow shirt to wear with the jeans she usually wore when the house was closed. She replaced the vase in the felt-lined basket and went to wash her hands in the stone sink.

'I thought we'd make the conventional tour, just as the visitors do,' she said, drying her hands. 'Then afterwards, if there's anything you want to see twice, we can retrace our steps. The cleaners have finished for today, Mr Mackenzie, so you can look your fill in peace.'

Alex Mackenzie stood his ground for a moment. 'Before we start, can I make a request?'

'Of course.' She waited politely.

'I prefer to use your first name,' he said bluntly. 'And I'd like you to use mine.'

'Then I shall.' She smiled. 'Let's make a start in the outer hall.'

Sarah did her best to forget that her charismatic male companion was anything other than one of the multitude of people who came to visit Ingham Lacey each year. And after a while her deep love for the house and her knowledge about every ornament and piece of furniture took over, communicating itself to the man, who listened and looked, making a comment now and then, asking a question at intervals, but who in the main seemed content to concentrate on the information his companion effortlessly provided as they made their tour of the ancient building, from the fourteenth-century crypt to the seventeenth-century drawing-room.

When the tour of the public section was over Sarah led the way to the private wing where Colonel and Mrs Newby had their living quarters.

'I thought you might like some tea,' she said, ushering him into a sitting-room furnished by the Edwardian owner of the house, with many modern comforts added since. Its welcoming air was in complete contrast to the austere beauty of the cordoned-off drawing-room, where every piece was unique and irreplaceable, and the cleaners were always heartily glad when their stint there was over. The beamed, low-ceilinged private sitting-room was furnished for comfort, with wide sofas and roomy chairs, tables with lamps and framed photographs, shelves full of books and curtains looped back to let every ray of sunlight in through the latticed windows.

'This is different—very warm and welcoming,' said Alex, halting on the threshold. 'The rest of the house is beautiful, but a bit on the dark side, even on a day like this.'

Sarah smiled ruefully. 'Light is the arch-enemy of conservation.'

'How do you cope with it?'

'We use covers a lot. Most of the furniture in great houses originally came with a complete set as part of the order. Fortunately a lot of these were intact for the things here. Leather covers for gilt and veneered furniture, heavy cotton for chairs and sofas, great bags for the chandeliers. And rooms were only opened when the family was in residence, remember. The rest of the time everything was covered and most of the rooms shut up, as it is here in winter, which is why so much of our heritage survives.'

Sarah excused herself to go to the kitchen, and swiftly made tea, then picked up the tray and went back to Alex, who was standing at one of the windows, looking out across the moat and the sunlit lawns to the stable block.

'It must be wonderful to live here,' he said, without turning round.

'It is. I never take it for granted.' Sarah put the tray down on a table in front of a sofa and sat down, feeling suddenly weary. The afternoon had been tiring, due mainly to her anxiety about the future plans for Ingham Lacey. And herself.

Alex crossed the room and sat beside her, accepted the cup of tea she gave him, but refused the cake Liz Wells had provided.

'I never eat sweet things,' he said, and looked at her closely. 'You look tired.'

Sarah shrugged, and drank some tea. 'I tend to get over-enthusiastic about the house. I hope you weren't bored by my outpourings.'

'On the contrary, I was enthralled.' He put down his cup. 'Right. Let's clear the air. I suppose everyone here is wondering why I'm spending time at Ingham Lacey, what my intentions, or the consortium's intentions, are regarding the property.'

Sarah nodded, mentally girding herself. 'Rumours are rife. Anything from a business centre to a Disney-style medieval theme park.'

Alex grimaced, laughing. 'I assure you,' he said, sobering, 'that nothing could be further from the truth.' He met her eyes squarely. 'The consortium—my father and myself most of all—feels that a building as old and rare as Ingham Lacey must be preserved in perpetuity for the general public, and that, in a nutshell, is the plan.

Nothing will be changed, other than in the interests of preservation of the house, and restoration, where necessary, will be done in as sympathetic a manner as possible. As I'm sure you know, my father has been in close contact with conservators right from the start, ten years ago, and any work done here will continue to be carried out discreetly, with as little disruption as possible to public viewing.'

Sarah sighed with a relief she made no attempt to hide. 'That's very good news.' She frowned. 'Then why, exactly, *are* you here? I can't believe that someone like you is spending a fortnight alone at the cottage—picturesque and charming though it is—just for a holiday.'

The gleam in his eyes intensified. 'Someone like me,' he repeated challengingly. 'Now what do you mean by that, I wonder?'

Sarah coloured. 'Merely that most of our clients are families, or couples.' She refilled their cups. 'It's very quiet here at Ingham Lacey.'

Alex drank the tea she gave him, eyeing her over the cup. 'In actual fact I'm very grateful for the breather. My job has sent me chasing all round the UK for the past year. I'm glad of some respite. When my father asked me to sort Ingham Lacey out I was only too glad to agree.'

'Sort out?' said Sarah with foreboding.

'Colonel Newby told me to put you in the picture as soon as possible,' said Alex, suddenly very businesslike. 'Needless to say all this has already been discussed with him. Mrs Newby, as you know, is finding it increasingly difficult, due to her arthritis, to cope with living at Ingham Lacey, but the Colonel wants to continue his job as custodian. My job is to provide a solution.'

Sarah looked at him intently. 'The Newbys have a house in Ingham village, so he could still continue in charge here without living in the private wing.'

'True. But from a security and insurance standpoint alone it's imperative that *someone* is in occupation of the house itself on a permanent basis.' He returned her look. 'That is the problem I'm here to sort out, without disturbing the status quo any more than I have to. Colonel Newby's father was my grandfather's commanding officer in World War Two, and for that reason alone we would wish him to continue. But, sentiment apart, the Colonel's a brilliant administrator, and runs the estate so efficiently that the consortium wants him to remain as custodian.'

'So how will you solve the problem?' asked Sarah.

'I'm not sure yet. Give me a chance.' He smiled. 'It's only twenty-four hours since I arrived. Don't worry. By the end of the fortnight I'll have everything under control.' He got up, holding out his hand. 'Thank you for your time today. You made the house come alive. It was an education to listen to you.'

Sarah rose to her feet and took the hand, rather surprised to find the palm hard and calloused. 'I was only too pleased,' she said, not quite truthfully. 'I hope I've been of some help.'

He kept her hand in his. 'You have. A great deal. Now, before I let you go, would you mind showing me the rest of the private wing?'

Sarah conducted him through the suite of rooms, all of them furnished with the same comfort and taste as the sitting-room, only this time she provided no running commentary, merely allowing Alex Mackenzie to explore at his own speed, and draw his own conclusions.

When he'd seen enough he thanked her again. 'I hope I haven't held you up too much. Will you finish cleaning that complicated vase before you knock off for the day?'

She nodded. 'It's a job to do when it's sunny and the light is good. The butler's pantry gets the best light in the house.'

'Your ally, in this instance, not your enemy!'

'True.' Sarah smiled at him. 'Thank you for putting me in the picture. No more nightmares about theme parks from now on.'

'Good. I was told you're the best housekeeper they've ever had here. It's in my interests to keep you happy. Goodbye for now.' He strolled from the room, and she heard his footsteps on the private stairway, then watched from the window as Alex emerged from the gatehouse, crossed the lawn to the cottage, and to her amusement ducked his head with practised ease as he went inside.

Back in the butler's pantry, the work of cleaning the second Derby vase was tedious for once, and Sarah, despite her euphoria at Alex's reassurances, was heartily glad when she'd returned the vases to the tables at either side of the fireplace in the drawing-room. When she'd made sure that all was secure for the night she returned to her own quarters, reminding herself that tonight she was going to cook a proper meal. To make sure she did, this morning she'd defrosted a salmon fillet and scrubbed some small new potatoes, so that now all she had to do was take a bath, put her dinner on to cook, and shell some broad beans Jack Selby had given her from his garden.

While she ate, Sarah mulled happily over Alex Mackenzie's revelations. She could sleep easily tonight. Suddenly it occurred to her that she hadn't asked permission to let the rest of the staff know. Jack and Liz Wells were just as concerned as she was, not to mention the Sewells. Poor Tim had envisaged all kinds of horrors being introduced into his beloved gardens.

Sarah drank some coffee, frowning thoughtfully, then cleared away her meal and ran upstairs to tidy herself up. She twisted her damp hair into a loose braid, put some lipstick on, then went downstairs, out of her front door and along the path to Alex Mackenzie's cottage. The lights were on, but a knock on the door brought no response and Sarah sighed, frustrated. She wanted permission to give Jack, and everyone else, the glad news.

Sarah went back to collect her basket and crossed the road to take in her laundry. As she carried her load back down the steep slope she noticed that Alex Mackenzie's car, a soft-top runabout that was rather less glamorous than she'd expected, was parked next to her own. So he hadn't gone far. As she crossed the road, she saw a tiny light glowing in the distance. Alex's cigar! She raced along the path to deposit her laundry inside her front door, then turned back and waited until he came in through the gate.

'Mr Mackenzie—Alex! Could you spare me a minute, please?'

'With the greatest of pleasure,' he said promptly. 'Good evening, Sarah. Will you come in for a drink?'

'Thank you.' Sarah went through the door he opened for her, stepping down into the room which looked rather more lived in than before, with several daily papers on the low table and an open book on the dented sofa cushions.

Alex smiled down at her, his pleasure in her company so openly displayed that Sarah felt a glow of warmth in response. 'I've got whisky, beer, even a couple of bottles of dry white wine on ice,' he informed her. 'What will you have?'

'A glass of wine would be perfect. Thank you.' Sarah watched with amusement as he stooped low to go through the doorway into the dining-room. He came back with glasses in one hand, an opened bottle of wine in the other and poured her a drink.

Sarah took it with a word of thanks, and plunged straight into her reason for speaking to him. 'I forgot to ask your permission to tell the others about your plans—or lack of them, to be more honest. Everyone's been anxious, as you can imagine.'

Alex smiled warmly. 'By all means pass on the news, Sarah. I intend talking to everyone in turn while I'm here, but in the meantime put as many minds at rest as you like.'

'That's wonderful!' Sarah smiled gratefully and sipped her wine. 'I'd been looking out for a new job. It's a relief to know I don't have to any more. Jobs like housekeeper at Ingham Lacey don't come up very often.'

He frowned. 'There was never any intention of making changes. How did the rumours start?'

She chuckled, feeling more relaxed by the minute. 'How does any rumour start? A lot of old houses need some kind of draw to bring in the crowds—motor museums and theme parks and so on. I suppose when the staff knew you were coming to stay they began speculating, and the speculation got wilder as it went along.'

Alex sat back, his eyes dancing. 'I must tell my father. I can just picture his reaction to a theme park! He loves this place as much as my grandfather did. Dad used to bring me here when I was a schoolboy. It was privately owned then, and you had to make an appointment to see over the place. These days he often drives down and wanders among the crowds. My mother prefers to come when there's a concert. She was under the weather the other night, so I used her ticket.'

'I suppose I must have met them both,' said Sarah, wondering how she could have missed a man who was probably an older version of Alex Mackenzie.

'You have.' He grinned. 'In fact my mother told me I'd be impressed by the housekeeper. Her little joke! I am impressed, of course, but I expected someone a lot older.'

'I'm thirty,' she said, looking into her glass. 'I believe the personnel arm of your consortium had doubts about my youth when I applied three years ago. But my qualifications met the requirements—an art history degree allied to a stint at a business college. And my fiancé was at school with one of your board members, so I suppose you could say strings were pulled quite hard.'

Alex's head went up at the word 'fiancé', and there was silence for an interval. With the curtains drawn and only a couple of the lamps lit, there was an intimacy to the low-ceilinged room that Sarah, who had chosen the furnishings herself, found wonderfully relaxing.

'Why did your fiancé pull strings to get you the job?' he asked, frowning. 'Was it his intention to work here too, in some capacity?'

'Oh, no. He's a university lecturer. I was one of his students.'

His frown deepened. 'But you said there was no man on the scene.'

'There isn't. Not any more.' She drank some of her wine.

'Would I be trespassing if I asked what happened?'

Sarah looked at him thoughtfully. 'No—not really.' She shrugged. 'The present Mrs Dryden was a student of his too. Martin got me the job as some kind of sop to his conscience because he wanted to marry Isobel instead.' She looked at the dark, disapproving face with some surprise. 'You must be extremely easy to talk to. Or the wine is uncommonly potent. One glass and I've poured out my life story. I do apologise.'

'Don't!' he said swiftly. 'I asked you a question and you answered, Sarah. Did you love this man?' He frowned. 'Sorry. Absolutely none of my business.'

Sarah shook her head. 'I can see why you're curious. I was certainly *in* love with Martin in the beginning. He's a good-looking intellectual with a brilliant brain and immense natural charm—a dangerous combination for one-to-one tutorials with worshipping young female students. He bowled me over so completely I dumped the current boyfriend and missed out on normal student social life,' she added regretfully.

Alex looked at her in silence for a moment. 'Were you engaged long?'

'Far too long. Martin was in no rush to get married. I was so young, he said. There was plenty of time to settle down.' Sarah grinned suddenly, her eyes dancing. 'Naïve, wasn't I? But I was eager to establish my own career, so I just thought he was encouraging my ambition. After my degree I went off to another college to do business studies. While I was otherwise employed, with only the occasional weekend with my betrothed to keep me going, my professor was basking in the warmth of his current admiration society, as usual.'

'Didn't you suspect?' asked Alex grimly, refilling her glass.

'Of course I did. But I told myself all that would change once we got married.' She shook her head. 'What a dope.'

'So what happened?'

'Isobel happened. She was different from the others, beautiful, but very much the intellectual, and—biggest difference of all—immune to the Dryden charm at first. But in the end the inevitable happened, only this time Martin fell desperately in love.'

Alex looked grim, obviously keeping quiet with effort.

'It was at this stage that the post came up here,' said Sarah without emotion. 'Martin pulled some old-school-tie strings to secure it for me in return for being such a sport about setting him free. Secretly I didn't feel at all sporting. I was livid.' Her eyes flashed at the memory. 'But Isobel was pregnant so I had no choice. I gave him back his ring and made myself scarce. Though to give him his due Martin really had cared for me—not in the way he does for Isobel, it's true, but enough to want to see me happy in a job he considered tailor-made for me.'

Alex smiled cynically. 'A prince among men.'

Sarah smiled, feeling oddly light-hearted. Reassurance about her job, and the added catharsis of talking about the erring Martin, left her feeling as though a great load had been taken off her shoulders. 'I've never told anyone all that before,' she said matter-of-factly.

'Your family?'

'They just know he wanted to marry someone else. At first my father wanted to beat Martin up, but my mother talked him out of it. She felt I had enough on my plate without that.'

'Pity,' said Alex casually. 'Which particular member of the board was your ex's schoolmate?'

'A man by the name of Nigel Bairstow. I didn't know him myself.'

'I do,' said Alex. 'Not a soul mate of mine.'

'He can't be a contemporary, either. Martin was—still is—twenty years older than me.'

'Do you feel bitter towards him?'

Sarah smiled a little. 'Not now. Eventually I could see we'd never been right for each other. And believe it or not I see quite a bit of Martin and Isobel. They've produced twins since young Jamie's arrival—fatherhood has changed Martin no end. Isobel writes successful, much acclaimed historical romance novels and he's given up the groves of Academe to be a kept man.'

'You're very magnanimous.' His eyes, which proved to be dark pewter-grey at close quarters, glittered coldly. 'I couldn't be, in the same circumstances.'

Sarah stood up. 'When I asked to speak to you for a minute I never imagined I'd be pouring all my woes in your ear. I'll hate myself in the morning.'

Alex got to his feet, smiling down at her. 'Please don't. I'm glad you came to see me. I was working up to asking you in for a drink. But I had the feeling you'd tell me it wasn't the done thing for the housekeeper of Ingham Lacey to fraternise with the holiday visitors.'

Sarah pulled a face. 'How right you are. I never have before. But then,' she added, 'you're not the usual holiday visitor, Mr Mackenzie.'

'*Alex*,' he said with emphasis. 'After tonight you can hardly retreat into formality. Besides, I flatly refuse to think of you as Miss Law.'

She gave him a sudden, mischievous smile. 'Jack and I are known as Law and Order by the staff, by the way.'

He chuckled. 'Are you such a martinet, then?'

'Slave-driver, according to some!' She sobered. 'Thank you for putting my fears at rest. I hated the thought of moving on.'

'As far as the consortium's concerned the job's yours as long as you want it,' he assured her. 'But surely you'll want to marry some day?'

'I seriously doubt that. It would have to be someone very special indeed to lure me away from Ingham Lacey.' Sarah held out her hand. 'Goodnight. I'm glad I took the bull by the horns and came to see you.'

'So am I.' Alex took her hand in his and held it for a moment. 'Come again. Any time.'

Sarah smiled, startled to find herself reluctant to leave. Alex opened the door for her and accompanied her along the path, said goodnight, then did her the courtesy of waiting deliberately until she was safe inside with her door locked.

CHAPTER THREE

SARAH saw nothing of her neighbour next day. During the period in which the house was open to the public she was on hand from eleven in the morning until five in the afternoon, in an atmosphere as sunny inside the house as the day outside once she'd given the glad news to Jack Wells and all the stewards.

By way of celebration, a euphoric Tim Sewell invited Sarah and Jack and Liz Wells round to share a barbecue with his family in the garden and take advantage of the still, perfect May evening. It was pleasant to sit in a deckchair and drink fruit punch, which Janet Sewell spiked with a tot of vodka once the junior Sewells had gone to bed. The only drawback to the evening was Sarah's sneaking feeling that it would have been better still with an escort of her own. Like Alex Mackenzie, perhaps.

That, she told herself, after Jack and Liz had walked her to her door, was pure fantasy. Alex Mackenzie was not for the likes of her. Almost the only thing she'd known about him before his arrival was his reputation with the opposite sex, via her sister, Jane. But until he'd made the reservation for the cottage, and the rumours began flying, she'd never given much thought to Alex Mackenzie, other than as the heir apparent to Mackenzie Holdings.

But it hadn't take her long to discover why he merited his reputation. Alex Mackenzie, without lifting a finger to do so, could charm the birds out of the trees. Sarah sniffed. And the last thing she needed in her life was a second run-in with a heartbreaker. Which made it all the more astonishing that she'd taken him into her confidence last night, telling him things she'd never confided to a soul. What in heaven's name had possessed her?

Feeling restless and out of sorts, Sarah stripped down to her T-shirt and curled up on the window seat in her bedroom to stare out at the night. The moon had set, but the sky was sequinned with stars, and the scent of lilac and hawthorne and newly cut grass came drifting up on the warm night air. She sat in darkness, conscious of a lack in her life she'd never felt since coming to Ingham Lacey. Not even after her break-up with Martin. Alex Mackenzie was to blame. This odd, immediate rapport with a man was something new in her life. And it worried her.

Suddenly she was aware of a new scent as cigar smoke drifted up on the still night air. Sarah leaned forward, craning her neck, and saw Alex leaning outside his door, cigar in hand. He sensed her presence, looked up, and saw the pale glimmer of her face in the dusk. He moved along the brick path until he stood directly beneath her open window.

'Come down,' he said softly, too low for the occupants of the other cottages to hear. 'Come over to the field; I need to see you urgently.'

Sarah pulled her jeans and sweater on over her T-shirt, thrust feet into espadrilles and ran downstairs with misgivings. Alex had already made his way across the road in the darkness, and she followed the will-o'-the-wisp of light of his cigar until she met him at the top of the field, out of sight and earshot of the cottages.

'What's wrong?' Sarah said breathlessly as she caught up with him.

'Nothing—now,' said Alex, and pulled her into his arms and kissed her hard.

Too astonished to protest, Sarah responded for a moment, then pulled herself together and gave a great shove, rocking him on his heels. 'Sorry, Mr Mackenzie,' she hissed, incensed. 'My contract doesn't include entertainment for the guests.' She turned on her heel, but Alex caught her hand, detaining her with a grasp she couldn't evade without an undignified tussle.

'I'm sorry. I apologise. I'll grovel, if you like. Blame the moon, the night, this fairy-tale place. I looked up at you at your window and—' He shrugged. 'Impulse isn't my style normally.'

Sarah calmed down a little. This man, she reminded herself, still had the power to dispense with her services if she offended him. 'Apology accepted. Goodnight.'

'Don't go,' he said imperiously, and moved nearer. Near enough for her to be conscious of warmth and good soap, tobacco and a faint tang of whisky, with none of the expensive aftershave Martin had favoured. Martin!

Her head went up. 'Would all this be due to the little story I told you last night, Mr Mackenzie? You can't know how much I regret telling you all that. My girlish confidences were a great mistake—you obviously think I need some physical consolation. Or,' she added with sudden suspicion, 'were you testing me, perhaps? Wondering if I was more friendly with some holiday guests than others?'

Alex dropped her hand as if it were a hot coal. 'No to both!' he said in disgust. 'I just wanted to kiss you. A fairly normal male instinct. I wanted to last night, too. As, Sarah Law, I think you well know. You're an intelligent, mature woman.'

'And your employee,' she reminded him without inflection.

The scented darkness crackled with sudden, added tension.

'And you actually think,' he said heavily after a while, 'that I'm the type to take advantage of that and demand some kind of droit du seigneur?'

'I've no idea, Mr Mackenzie. I'm just making it clear that, much as I love my job, there are certain things I won't do to keep it.'

The words seemed to hang in the air between them and, feeling suddenly weary and depressed, and wondering why she'd made such a fuss, Sarah turned away, and went down the sloping field in such a hurry that she stumbled awkwardly, and the wooden seat of the swing thumped her in the back and sent her sprawling.

'Sarah!'

Almost before she'd come to a stop on the slope she was scooped up into powerful arms. Alex carried her back to the house at top speed, dumped her on her sofa and went down on his knees to run hard, questing hands over her.

'Are you in pain?' he demanded urgently, his face grim as his fingers probed through her hair.

Sarah pushed him away and sat upright. 'The only thing damaged is my dignity!' she assured him. Their eyes met, she bit her lip, then suddenly both of them began to laugh.

'Midsummer madness comes early,' said Alex ruefully when he'd sobered. 'No other excuse.'

'You said you needed to see me urgently,' she reminded him, removing bits of grass from her hair.

'I did. I showed you why. I saw you in the window, Rapunzel in her tower, and because I knew damn well you wouldn't let me in I lured you out.' His eyes, glittering like silver in the lamplit room, held hers steadily. 'It was nothing more sinister than a need to celebrate this wonderful night with a kiss under the stars.' He pulled a face, his wide, mobile mouth expressing his amusement. 'You've discovered my secret—I'm a closet romantic. Don't give me away, please!'

Sarah grinned. 'I won't.'

'You could always keep it in mind—use it as blackmail some day,' he said, his voice a tone deeper as he moved nearer.

Sarah knew he wanted to kiss her again, something she wanted just as much. Which was a problem. After her outraged protest in the field she could hardly melt in compliance now that they were indoors. 'Won't you get up, Alex? You're still on your knees.'

He got up in a swift, economical movement, but only to sit beside her. 'I'm Alex again,' he commented, and began combing his fingers through her hair to remove more grass. 'Sarah, just for a moment could you forget that either of us has anything to do with Ingham Lacey?'

'Why?' she asked, trying to ignore the tremors running through her at his touch.

'You know why,' he said sternly, and took her in his arms and kissed her. When she offered no resistance Alex drew her close, coaxing her lips apart to let in his caressing tongue. He made no attempt to caress her otherwise, only the tightening of his arms betraying the urgency which surged up inside him as their kisses grew wilder and their breathing ragged. At last Alex let her go with reluctance, kissed the top of her tousled head, trailed a hand down her cheek, then stood up, met her eyes for a long, silent moment, and without a word left the cottage and went back to his own.

Alex Mackenzie's slow, controlled lovemaking proved to be the disastrous prelude to a bad night's sleep. Sarah tossed and turned in her bed half the night, cursing the effect Alex had on her. Last night she'd told him the story of her life. Tonight she'd let him kiss her senseless. If Alex was a closet romantic, so, it seemed, was she. The night, the stars, the scents of summer, the unrecognised clamouring of her own hormones had all combined to make her restless and in need of something she hadn't even known she wanted until Alex Mackenzie had kissed her. But tonight they'd been simply a man and a woman who found each other attractive and had acted on it. Tomorrow she would be Miss Law, the housekeeper of Ingham Lacey, again, and Alex Mackenzie would be, as he had been all along, the consortium's representative.

Sarah found she had no cause for concern. The house was closed to the public next day, and when she arrived there to supervise the cleaning of the new chapel she found Alex Mackenzie with Jack Wells, deep in consultation with the foreman of the builders engaged in restoration work on the south-east wall.

Alex turned as she drew near, giving her a friendly smile. 'Good morning, Miss Law. Lovely day again.'

'Good morning, Mr Mackenzie. Good morning, Jack.' She felt light-headed with relief. Last night, it was plain, was last night. Today they were on a business footing again. And would stay there, too, she decided. Much as she'd enjoyed the experience, dalliance with the boss was a bad idea all round.

'I've had a thought, Jack,' she said, smiling, including Alex in the conversation. 'If you'd like to spend time at home for a couple of nights I'll sleep in the house. Liz must be tired of having you dash off after dinner all the time.'

Jack looked surprised. 'You mean that, Sarah?'

'Very much so. If Ned Frome comes visiting I shan't mind,' she assured him, aware that Alex knew exactly why she was offering.

'Who's Ned Frome?' he asked.

'A young Cavalier who hid here during the Civil War,' said Jack. 'The lad was wounded, so the ladies of the house stuck him in the priest-hole. Unfortunately the Roundheads came to search the house and no one could get back to him for hours. By the time they did he was dead. According to legend he haunts the place.'

'And you won't mind that?' said Alex to Sarah.

'No,' she assured him. 'Ghosts don't bother me at all. And there's a very complex alarm system to deal with flesh-and-blood intruders. I'll be happy to take over for a night or two, Jack.' Safer, too, she thought, than succumbing to any more midsummer madness.

'If you do get an intruder don't hesitate to call for help,' said Alex, poker-faced. 'I'll come running.'

'We're on a direct line to the police,' Jack assured him, plainly wanting to take advantage of Sarah's offer. 'And Sarah's got a mobile phone. Help could arrive within minutes if she needed it.'

'It's settled, then,' she said briskly. 'Duty calls; I must go, gentlemen.'

The rest of Sarah's day was spent, as always when the house was closed, supervising the scrupulous, endless cleaning process that went on behind the scenes. Four women alone were needed to keep the panelling free from dust, and on this occasion one of them was off sick. Sarah filled in, glad of the company and the laborious work as an antidote to dwelling on Alex Mackenzie.

When the working day was over Sarah went back to the cottage, had a long bath, made herself a quick meal, then packed a bag, locked up and went back to the house. She strolled towards it slowly, content just to look at it. Ingham Lacey always looked fabulously beautiful as the sun was setting—like an illustration from a fairy tale. She stopped to chat with Tim and Janet Sewell as they watered the flowerbeds, then met the couple from the holiday cottage, out with their baby for an evening stroll before bedtime. Sarah admired the diminutive Emma, exchanged a few pleasantries, then went over the drawbridge, through the gatehouse and up the winding stone stair to the private apartments.

Someone, Jack probably, had left all the lights burning despite the bright evening outside. Sarah smiled. She had told the truth about her lack of nerves when it came to ghosts, but Jack's thoughtfulness was very welcome just the same. And here in the house, even though the drawbridge could no longer be hauled up to keep out the enemy, she was safe. Alex Mackenzie was a dangerously exciting man. The sooner he was away from Ingham Lacey the better.

Sarah rang her parents for a chat, read a little, and was on the point of going early to the comfortable bed in the apartment guest room when her mobile phone rang. She picked it up, thinking it was Jack, then stif-

fened as she heard a voice which, even after o.
days' acquaintance, she would have known anywh

'Are you all right?' asked Alex Mackenzie.

'Yes, of course,' she returned coolly.

'I can't help feeling I'm to blame.'

'What for, exactly?'

'For your night alone in that haunted old house.'

'I like it here. It's peaceful.'

'And free from threat of intrusion.'

'Your words, not mine.'

'But it's why you're there, Sarah. You're afraid your next-door neighbour will get too familiar.'

In point of fact he was wrong. It was herself she was afraid of. 'Not at all. I merely felt Jack would like a night or two in his own bed.'

'Having met Mrs Wells, I can sympathise with that! But Sarah,' he added quickly, 'will you just take down my phone number? Key it in on your phone, so you can just press a number if you want me. I can be over there in seconds.'

'There's no need—really. I've got Jack's number, and Tim's.'

'Both of whom could do with a good night's rest,' Alex interrupted. 'If you need anyone call *me*. Here's the number.'

Sarah stiffened at the hint of command in his tone, but quickly scribbled the number he gave her on a note-pad. 'There,' she said afterwards. 'I've got it, but you won't be disturbed, I promise. I've slept here before. I'm not the least bit nervous.'

'About ghosts I believe it. But a human intruder's a different story. If anyone's misguided enough to break in don't, whatever you do, try to deal with it yourself,' he ordered.

'I've been properly trained to deal with emergencies,' Sarah assured him tartly. 'Now I'll just take advantage of the peace and quiet and have an early night. But Alex,' she added with sudden contrition, 'thank you. It's very thoughtful of you.'

'Not at all,' he assured her. 'I told you I was a secret romantic. If you're in distress at any time I absolutely insist on charging to your rescue.'

Sarah laughed, wished him goodnight, then put down the phone feeling rather pleased with life.

She slept at the house for two nights, but neither Jack nor Liz would hear of her staying there longer.

'Liz says she feels guilty enough as it is,' Jack declared on the third morning as they were opening up the house to the public. 'You go back to your own little nest tonight, Sarah. But thanks. I miss my own bed.'

Sarah told Jack she'd been only too happy to change places for a bit, then went on with her day until the house closed for the night and she was free to make her way back through the overcast evening to her cottage. It was warm and sultry and, if the sky was anything to go by, shaping up for a storm. On the way back she knocked on the Hendersons' door, reminding them that if there was a power failure torches were stored in the broom cupboard.

'No candles, I'm afraid,' she said in apology. 'We can't have naked lights in these old buildings—the fire risk is too great.'

The young couple assured her they would take care, and as Sarah turned away with a friendly goodnight she saw Alex leaning in the doorway of the main cottage.

'Hello, there,' she said brightly. 'Perhaps I'd better repeat my warnings to you too. We provide torches, but no matches or candles, please, if we get a power cut.'

'I'd worked that one out for myself,' he said with a grin, and grimaced as he looked round at the beamed, low-ceilinged room behind him. 'This old place would go up like a torch.'

'I had to repeat my warning,' she pointed out. 'It's my job.'

'I know. And very well you do it too.' His grin twisted a little. 'Glad to be home?'

'Yes. I love my little house. But I enjoyed a change of scene for a couple of nights.' She smiled at him serenely, and went along the path to her own front door.

After the spacious rooms of the apartment in the house, her little cottage seemed smaller than usual, but cosily familiar and very much her own. Only it wasn't really, Sarah reminded herself. It belonged to Mackenzie Holdings, and she was only here as long as she held down the job of housekeeper. And getting on over-friendly terms with Alex Mackenzie was the wrong way to make sure she did. From now on she would keep him at arm's length. Pity, though, she admitted wistfully.

The storm arrived in due course, but there was no power cut, to Sarah's relief. For a while it was very noisy in the peaceful valley which sheltered Ingham Lacey, but by bedtime the rain had stopped, the lightning was just a pretty display of fireworks in the distance and the thunder had rolled away towards London. She sat at her window seat, breathing in the smell of hot, damp earth, watching the clouds clear to let the stars come out, glad there'd been no storm while she'd slept at the house.

Nor, she thought, with a grin, had poor Ned Frome come to haunt her, bloodstains on his ruffled shirt and satin breeches. Which, according to legend, was how he'd appeared to those who swore they'd seen him. Since this description, minus the bloodstains, was identical to a portrait in the house of a young heir in Stuart times, Sarah refused to believe a word of it.

As Sarah was leaving the cottage next morning Alex, dressed in running vest and jogging pants, intercepted her as she crossed the garden.

'Sarah, good morning. Are you very busy today?'

She gave him what she hoped was a friendly, impersonal smile. 'Good morning. The house is closed today, so I'm doing the usual sort of thing. Why? Is there something I can do for you?'

'I'd like to take you out to lunch. Purely business,' he added hastily. 'There's something I want to discuss.'

Sarah thought for a moment. The cleaning team was well able to function without her. And she was due some time off. 'I need to work in the house until at least eleven,' she said crisply. 'I could be free by twelve. Will that do?'

Alex smiled, his eyes gleaming with something she rather thought was triumph. Had he expected her to refuse? If so perhaps she should have done.

'Perfect. I'll knock on your door. I'm off for a run through the lanes; see you later.' He gave her a wave and set off for the gate with easy, graceful strides. Sarah, controlling a desire to watch him out of sight, went off to occupy herself as fully as possible until she could decently leave her labours and go home to make an attack on her appearance. Whatever Alex Mackenzie had to say to her, she wanted to look her best to listen to it.

CHAPTER FOUR

SARAH'S announcement that she was taking a few hours off met with warm approval from her staff. Feeling like a child let out of school, she went back to her cottage mid-morning and spent an enjoyable hour achieving the best possible result with the raw materials nature had given her.

The experience with Professor Martin Dryden had dented Sarah's self-esteem quite disastrously after the break-up. For a while her interest in clothes and appearance was nil, and she abandoned the expensive short haircut Martin liked so much. By the time her clothes consciousness had revived again her taste had changed, to timeless and classic rather than the latest whims of fashion, and her dark red hair had grown to the length she now kept it to from choice. It brushed her shoulders on the rare occasions she left it loose, but Sarah invariably wore it in a knot or braided coil as more suited to the title 'housekeeper'.

Sarah washed and brushed her hair until it gleamed like mahogany, then secured it at the nape of her neck with an intricate silver filigree clasp that Jane had brought back from a holiday in Goa. After a look at the sunlit day outside she put on a long, full-skirted dress of thin biscuit lawn patterned with small, blurred flowers in cream and burnt orange. Fawn leather sling-backs, thin silver hoops in her ears, and Sarah was ready for the knock which sounded on her door a minute or two before she was expecting it. Not a man to keep one waiting, Alex Mackenzie. Pretty sure that he equally approved of punctuality in others, Sarah threw open the door and smiled, secretly highly gratified by the admiration in his eyes.

'You look wonderful,' Alex said without preamble, looking good to Sarah himself in a cream shirt and chinos, an oatmeal cotton sweater knotted about his shoulders. 'I'm told there's a pub called the Pheasant about ten miles away, deep in the heart of leafy Kent. Don't worry,' he added as he handed her into his car. 'Jack Wells drew a diagram—it's on the dashboard.'

'Am I to navigate?' asked Sarah as he got in. 'I warn you, I've never been to the place myself.'

'I've got complete trust in your capabilities,' he returned firmly, and nosed the car out into the narrow lane. 'Right, then, Sarah Law, start navigating.'

They reached their goal without a hitch, threading their way down a maze of turnings down improbably narrow lanes, and discovered that the Pheasant was a very inviting little inn, old and beamed, with tubs of flowers and tables outside under an awning and already well patronised by only a little after midday. Sarah settled herself happily at one of the outside tables to look at a vista of green, sheep-inhabited fields while Alex went inside to fetch drinks. This was an unexpected treat, she thought, relaxing. Though there was no earthly reason why she couldn't bring herself to places like this in her time off. Not that it was quite the same thing to come alone. An escort like Alex Mackenzie made a world of difference.

He returned with brimming glasses of ice-cold lager, two large menus tucked under his arm. He sat beside her with a sigh of pleasure, clinked glasses, then took a long pull of his drink.

'This,' he said with satisfaction, 'is my idea of a place to eat. I don't care if the food isn't good. The company—' he made her a small bow '—and the surroundings are enough.'

Sarah smiled as she studied the dishes on offer. 'By the look of this I think the food might match the rest of it.'

'Jack assures me that the beef and oyster pie is first-class.'

'Then you can be sure it is. Jack likes his food!'

They pondered at length over the choices, debating the merits of the pie against hot king-sized prawns with Szechuan sauce.

'I get in such a mess trying to get the shells off,' said Sarah, pulling a face.

'Does it matter?' said Alex lazily.

'No. Not in the least.' She laughed. 'Just ask for extra napkins.'

Sarah's prawns arrived with the required napkins, plus a finger bowl of hot water, and she set to with gusto, the entire process of shelling and sucking out the succulent flesh an antidote to constraint. Alex displayed none whatsoever, but Sarah had found it hard to dismiss the memory of their last private exchange entirely until now. While he demolished his flaky, golden work of art, making noises of appreciation over the contents, Sarah worked her way through the prawns and the creative salad she was served with them, enjoying herself enormously as the conversation flowed between them with the ease of longer acquaintance than theirs.

Alex wanted to know every last detail of the work she did at Ingham Lacey, and, after Sarah told him in brief, gave her in return an idea of his role with Mackenzie Holdings.

'I qualified as an architect, but I function these days as a sort of troubleshooter. I visit all the concerns in turn, make sure they're all functioning to the height of their potential, and, if not, put forward plans and suggestions for improvement.'

'Do you stay to see they're carried out?' asked Sarah, impressed.

'Mostly. Sometimes it's something so minimal I don't need to. Other times I spend up to six months with them, even more, to make sure the new idea is implemented.' Alex shrugged. 'Which is why my flat in town feels more like a hotel room than a home. For some time now I've had a move in mind. I want a place that welcomes me when I do get home. At present I only get that with my parents'.'

Sarah pushed her debris-filled plate away, and mopped vigorously with damp paper napkins. 'Anywhere in mind?' she asked, sitting back with a sigh. 'Thank you for the meal. It was delicious—and I was hungry.'

'I could tell,' he said with a laugh, then eyed her with a hint of challenge. 'I do have a place in mind. It's part of the reason why I asked you here today. To discuss it.'

'Really? Why me?' said Sarah, frowning. 'I know nothing about London property.'

Alex paused while a girl came to clear their plates away, then he sat back, long legs outstretched, his eyes on the view. 'My idea—if it meets with approval—is to kill two birds with one stone. The simplest solution to the problem of a tenant for Ingham Lacey is to move in myself.'

Sarah turned her head sharply, astounded. 'Are you serious?'

'Never more so.' He met her look challengingly. 'Would you object?'

'No—of course not. But it's not really anything to do with me.'

Alex shook his head. 'You love Ingham Lacey, Sarah. I know that. I've been over the place a lot lately—you must have noticed me.'

'Oh, yes,' she said drily. 'I noticed. You're pretty hard to miss.'

He smiled, fine laughter wrinkles fanning at the corners of his eyes. 'I stick out like a sore thumb among the visitors, you mean.'

'No. But somehow your presence makes itself felt. I'm not the only one who feels that. All the Ingham Lacey staff are speculating on your intentions—' Sarah blew out her cheeks. 'Though no one had the faintest idea you meant to live there yourself.'

'My original aim was to see how conservation and restoration could be made easier—if more people were needed to take care of it,' he went on, looking out over the fields again. 'But you run the place on oiled wheels. I was told there are people in the village you can call on as back-up if any of your helpers are ill, and that you, personally, take on projects during the winter, like cleaning the armour and doing some restoration on the paintings and so on.'

'You've obviously spent a lot of time with Jack Wells,' said Sarah.

'What I'm trying to say is that nothing needs improvement. I think Tim Sewell could do with another team member, and if there's anything—or anyone—you need to make *your* life easier you have only to say so.'

There was silence for a moment, then Sarah said slowly, 'I've taken courses in restoration, both in college and during my time at Ingham Lacey, but only with ceramics and paintings. I could use a skilled needlewoman for the hangings in the Chinese bedroom. That's not my field. But otherwise I think we're a pretty well-knit team.'

'So do I.' Alex slanted a look at her. 'You still haven't commented on my idea of making this a base for myself.'

For good reason. His statement had utterly floored her. Alex Mackenzie on hand for a period of two weeks was a different kettle of fish from having him as a semipermanent part of Ingham Lacey.

'If you mean to live here,' Sarah began, 'what happens when you're away? You say you are quite a lot.'

'Most Mackenzie holdings are situated within reach of London, which means they're also within easy commuting distance of Ingham Lacey,' he said crisply. 'If I had a home I wanted to return to I would make it my business to be there a great deal more than I am in my present place. And when I wasn't I'm sure that you and the staff at Ingham Lacey could make up some kind of rota to see that someone sleeps in the house while I'm away. Think about it,' he added, 'while I order some coffee.'

Sarah watched his broad-shouldered figure disappear into the inn, then returned her attention to the landscape in front of her. Now that she was getting used to the idea she was, she admitted, rather gratified that Alex Mackenzie had done her the courtesy of bringing her to lunch to tell her about his plan. Not that her approval was necessary. If the consortium approved Alex's plans it wouldn't make an iota of difference whether she liked the idea or not. But now she had time alone to consider it she did like it. She liked it a lot.

'That's a very intent look,' he commented as he came back with two steaming cups. 'It's busy in there. It was simpler to bring these myself.'

'Thank you,' she said abstractedly, and stirred sugar into her coffee.

'Well?' he demanded. 'Have you come to any conclusion?'

'Yes.' She turned to look at him. 'I've decided it was very good of you to bring me here to tell me your plans. Because neither my approval or disapproval is of the slightest importance, really, is it?'

'Actually you're wrong,' he said shortly. 'If I move in I would like to do so with your wholehearted sanction. I know the house means a lot to you. But it *owes* a lot to you too. Only tender loving care of the variety you administer—and inspire—could keep it in its present state of perfection.'

'It's kind of you to say so.'

'It's the truth.'

Sarah put an end to his suspense. 'I saw the way you looked that evening, when you were standing at the window in the private sitting-room. I think you're as smitten with the place as I am. I hope you'll be very happy living there.'

Alex's face relaxed. 'Thank you, Sarah. I know I will be—now.' He got up, holding out his hand. 'There's a footpath over the road. Let's walk.'

Sarah let him help her over the stile and lift her down onto a path paved with mud baked hard by the sun, with tree roots forming steps and obstacles at intervals. The footpath was narrow, with a hedge and trees on one side, a fence on the other, enclosing a field full of Jacob sheep. The animals moved away in umbrage at the intrusion, and stood in indignant groups, waiting until the humans had passed by. The sun was high, but in the shelter of the trees it was cool and shaded and Sarah strolled abreast with Alex sometimes, at others obliged to go ahead where the path narrowed. After a while it began to plunge quite steeply and Alex took her hand, his smile wry as he noted her shoes.

'Sorry, I didn't realise it was so steep.'

For answer Sarah stooped and removed her shoes, dangling them by their straps from her free hand as she went barefoot along the hard-packed path, liking the feel of the silky dust beneath the soles of her feet.

'I can hear water,' she said as the descent grew steeper, and to her delight found that the footpath led them to a small stream which rushed over mossy stones under trees which leaned over it to form a green, vaulted roof, shading them from the sun. They had been walking for less than fifteen minutes, yet suddenly they were in a quiet, private world, the silence broken by nothing other than the plash of water and the sound of some kind of farm machinery, whirring lazily in the distance.

Alex spread his sweater over a space between tree roots on the mossy bank and lowered her down on it, then settled himself beside her.

'It's strange,' he said abruptly.

'What is?' she said idly, leaning back against the tree, her eyes dreamy as she watched the hypnotic tumble of water.

'How extraordinarily comfortable I feel with you. I met you precisely six days ago, yet I feel as though I've known you for years.'

Sarah laughed. 'Comfortable! If that's a compliment it's a first for me.' She gave him a sidelong glance. 'Perhaps we met in some former incarnation.'

'If so, what were we to each other, I wonder?'

'You were the lord of the manor and I was one of your serfs,' she said promptly.

'More likely the other way round.' His voice deepened as he took her hand and held it loosely, one finger smoothing the back of it. 'Of course, we could have been equals, just as we are now.'

'But we're not. You *are* lord of the manor, more or less. And if not your serf exactly, I'm still just the housekeeper.'

His fingers tightened with sudden ferocity. 'You're not *just* anything, Sarah Law. Housekeeper of Ingham Lacey is hardly a menial occupation. These past days, as I've been going over the place, my mind has reeled with the complexity of what you deal with. Don't sell yourself short.'

'But I don't.' She detached her hand. 'I'm very proud of what I do.'

They looked at each other in a silence which lengthened, and Sarah sat very still as she watched the grey eyes darken almost to black. She felt suddenly precarious, endangered, as though she were on the edge of an abyss and about to fall in.

Which was nonsense, Sarah told herself, and sat up-right, but Alex put a hand on her shoulder and gently pushed her back against the tree.

'Stay still,' he commanded in a voice so soft and deep that her heart gave a great lurch. 'You look like a dryad, or a water nymph, unreal—'

'But I'm not unreal,' she said firmly, and got up in a hurry, then wished she hadn't as he leapt up, caught her in his arms and held her fast.

'You can't know how much I regretted kissing you that night,' he said rapidly, 'or that I have trouble in sleeping because I want so badly to do it again, and much, much more than that—' His lips were on hers before they could open in protest, her resistance crushed by arms which tightened round her like a vice.

Then voices sounded from the far side of the stream, and Sarah thrust him away, gasping. She snatched up her shoes just as a party of hikers came into view along the path. There was an exchange of greetings as they drew level and passed on, leaving a fraught silence behind them.

'Hell,' said Alex bitterly, and caught her hand in his. 'No. Don't pull away.'

Sarah glared at him, her eyes blazing. 'Did you bring me along here for the sole purpose of—of—?'

'Making love to you?' he finished for her. 'No. I didn't. It just happened.'

'Fun and games in the woods is a pastime I left behind with puberty,' she snapped.

'Pity.' His mouth twisted. 'But don't go yet. Stay with me a little longer, Sarah. Please,' he added, as such an obvious afterthought that she thawed a little in amusement, then nodded, privately disapproving of her own weakness, but well aware that moments of privacy with Alex Mackenzie would be out of the question once he took up residence at the house. And a good thing too, she thought bleakly. She leaned back against the tree, her eyes on the water rushing over the mossy stones as she chose the words that had to be said.

'The job description in my contract,' she began, 'doesn't exactly state that my conduct must be above reproach, like Caesar's wife. But it's implicit in the text just the same. I occupy a position of trust. Any relationship with you, other than a purely business arrangement, is out of the question.'

Alex gave her a brooding sidelong glance. 'Which means that if I come to live in the private quarters the only contact with you must be purely professional?'

'I'm afraid so.'

He gave a short, mirthless laugh. 'You at least have the grace to sound sorry.'

'I am,' she said honestly.

'Does that mean you didn't object to the kiss on a purely personal basis?'

She hesitated, and Alex turned and pulled her into his arms. 'In that case I might as well compound the felony,' he said huskily, and kissed her with a tenderness which put an end to her resistance. A great shiver ran through his body as he felt her yield to him, and he tightened his arm around her waist, his free hand sliding over her breasts, burning through the flimsy fabric of her dress. She felt heat rush through her like an electric shock and gasped as he bent to kiss her throat, his clever, practised fingers delicately relentless, arousing her to such a new, undreamed-of response that she could hardly bear it.

Then abruptly she was free. It was over. He moved back a fraction and Sarah felt as though she'd been dropped from a great height as they stared at each other, breathing raggedly in painful, uneven gasps, Alex's eyes boring into hers.

'This is impossible,' he said harshly. 'I want you and you know it. And you feel something for me too. Do you deny it?'

Sarah shook her head, and turned away from the heat in his eyes.

'Then what shall we do about it?' he demanded.

There was a long silence, broken only by the rushing water and the breeze rustling the leaves overhead.

'Nothing,' said Sarah at last.

Alex seized her hands in his, spinning her to face him. He stared down at her incredulously. '*Nothing?* What do you mean? Are you telling me I imagined all that?'

She shook her head. 'No.'

'You know perfectly well,' he said hotly, 'that if we'd been somewhere else, in private, with no one likely to disturb us, I couldn't have let you go. I want you, Sarah, and I give you fair warning—I mean to have you.'

'Oh, do you?' She glared at him, jerking her hands away to push her hair back behind her ears—an early warning sign that her family would have recognised with foreboding. 'How many times do I have to say it's out of the question? Can you imagine how the rest of the staff at Ingham Lacey would react if it was known I was indulging in fun and games with the heir apparent to Mackenzie Holdings?'

'Stop demeaning it like that!' he snapped, enraged. 'It may have been a game to you, Sarah Law. For me it was making love.'

'You mean lust, not love!'

Alex's eyes glittered coldly, in disturbing contrast to the molten heat of seconds before. 'I know exactly what I meant,' he said, his voice dangerously quiet. 'I shall demonstrate the difference.' He pushed her back against the tree, imprisoning her against it, her flailing hands caught fast in one of his as he held her against the rough bark with the weight of his body.

Sarah choked an outraged protest, trying to twist free, but Alex held her still, grinding his mouth into hers, handling her in insulting parody of the caresses minutes earlier as the kiss went on and on until she thought she would suffocate. Suddenly Alex released her, stepped back and stared at her in cold, derisive amusement, breathing hard but otherwise, to Sarah's rage, apparently unmoved.

'*That* was lust. A little lesson for you, Sarah Law,' he said bitingly. 'It doesn't do to push the male animal too far. It might have been possible with your tame professor. I'm a different proposition.'

Sarah stood straight, detaching a twig from her hair. 'Very different,' she agreed acidly. 'Martin came from a working-class family with very little money to help him with his education. He got where he did by hard work and scholarships. You were born to money.'

Alex eyed her with dislike. 'I might have been born into comfortable circumstances, but I was trained from birth not to take them for granted. Why do you think I'm built like a coal-heaver? Not because I work out at trendy gymnasiums, believe me, but because I've been expected to do everything that the lowliest employees do at any one of the companies under the Mackenzie umbrella. In my university vacations I've been a labourer, hod-carrier, brickie on different building sites—brick-layer to you,' he added cuttingly. 'I can wield a shovel with the best of them. I even learnt to service heavy goods vehicles before my required stint of driving them for the company, qualified architect or not.

'In short, Miss Law, I may have had the security of a job all my life, but I damn well had to work my socks off to prove I was worthy of it.' He bent to pick up his sweater. 'Right. If you're ready I'll drive you back.'

CHAPTER FIVE

THE journey back to Ingham Lacey was made in fraught silence for a while, except for the occasional road direction from Sarah. But as her anger subsided depression set in. She had offended Alex very badly; that was obvious. Her use of the word lust had been a deadly insult to the romantic who lurked behind the tough, efficient exterior, and his retaliation had been instinctive, born of a furious need to teach her a lesson. A man like Alex Mackenzie would be accustomed to a very different reaction to his lovemaking. And, to be fair, she could understand why. He was very good at it. Much better than Martin. Sarah bit her lip at the thought and stole a look at his taut profile, surprised to meet a swift, sidelong glance from eyes which were no longer as cold and hard as the pewter they resembled.

Alex steered the car into a layby and killed the engine, then released his seat belt and turned to look at her, his mouth tightening at the hostility on her face.

'Don't worry, I shan't jump on you again.'

Sarah looked at him levelly. 'Good.'

'I apologise for what I did back there,' he said stiffly.

'You were angry.'

'Which is no excuse.' He thrust a hand through his thick, curling hair, his eyes holding hers. 'Will you agree to a truce, Sarah?'

For a moment she was tempted to lash out at him, tell him to get lost. But common sense prevailed. He was part of the consortium which employed her.

'If you're really going to come and live at the house,' she said evenly, 'it would be inconvenient to remain at loggerheads with each other.'

His mouth twisted in a wry smile. 'Particularly when it's the last thing I want. Let's start again,' he added, surprising her.

Sarah's eyebrows rose, and he held up a hand.

'I meant, Sarah, that perhaps we could get to know each other better, little by little. As must be patently obvious, you appeal to me strongly. In more ways than just your looks,' he added quickly. 'I feel a rapport with you I've never experienced with a woman before. So much so that I lost my temper back there because you read me wrong. Caveman tactics are not normally my style.'

Probably, Sarah thought, because he'd never had to resort to them before. 'I'm sure they're not.'

Alex looked at her gravely. 'Thank you.' He fastened his seat belt and started the car. 'When we get back would you ask everyone to come to the Great Hall before they leave for the day, Sarah? It's time I made an official statement.'

Not long afterwards he drove into the field reserved for the stable block car park, stopped the car, then put a hand on hers as she made to get out. 'But Sarah, I meant what I said.'

'In which particular instance?' she queried, her poise restored now she was back on familiar ground.

'For now I'll settle for friendship,' he said with emphasis, 'but eventually I want more than that. I give you fair warning.'

Sarah, still smarting from the rough little lesson at his hands, looked at him very directly. 'I obviously gave out the wrong signals at some stage, Alex. Friendship I'd like. But it's the only thing on offer.'

He smiled, undismayed. 'We'll see. In the meantime would you please ask everyone to turn up at six for my talk? I won't keep them long.'

Sarah went into her cottage with mixed feelings, one of which was relief at having time to spend alone before going over to the house. She stood under a cool shower for some time, her hair wrapped in a towel. Afterwards she dressed in a tailored green linen skirt and green-striped white shirt, twisted her hair up into a knot, did her face and went outside to cross the manicured green lawn to the house. Swiftly she went from room to room, passing on Alex's message, using her mobile phone to contact the outside staff.

At six precisely she joined the others in the Great Hall, a second or two before Alex Mackenzie arrived. He too had changed from his casual elegance of earlier, into a lightweight suit and formal shirt and tie. He directed a friendly smile all round then launched into a confirmation of his plans to live in the private quarters of the house, giving his reassurance that otherwise the consortium intended Ingham Lacey to continue exactly as before.

'With just one difference,' he added. 'Since I shall be on the spot regularly, either Colonel Newby, Miss Law or Jack Wells can report any problems or suggestions directly to me. My father's wish, as I said before, is to ensure that future generations can continue to enjoy the valuable piece of history that is Ingham Lacey. It's a fragile old building, but with your help and vigilance we're determined to make every effort to preserve it.'

The approval on all sides was expressed with fervour as everyone clustered round Alex Mackenzie to express their appreciation.

'So it's official, then,' said Jack Wells in an undertone to Sarah.

She nodded. 'Though to be honest I wonder if Mr Mackenzie has any idea how cold it can be here in winter. It's pretty cool in here now, Jack, and this is May.'

'The private rooms are warmer, though, Sarah. And to give the chap his due he doesn't look the type to worry about a bit of cold weather.'

Sarah raised a noncommittal eyebrow, then smiled as Alex came towards them, the others having taken their leave.

'That went very well.'

He met her smiling look head-on. 'I thought it best for everyone to know the exact nature of my intentions.'

Sarah's eyes dropped before the message in his, and she excused herself swiftly to lock up for the night. 'I'll see to everything, Jack. You get off home to Liz, or it'll soon be time to get back for the night.'

As she left the Great Hall, straight-backed, Sarah knew very well that Alex watched her out of sight, pleased that he'd forced her to retreat.

Life at Ingham Lacey proceeded without incident, though Sarah encountered Alex often enough, as was inevitable, since he took great interest in every part of the function of the house. He was on easy terms with everyone, managing to combine authority and assurance with a brisk friendliness that was much appreciated by all, especially the older lady stewards, who were loud in their praise of young Mr Mackenzie every time they spoke to Sarah. Also, it was impossible to live next door to someone without frequent accidental encounters.

But Sarah made very sure there was no opportunity for any more midsummer madness. If she had laundry to hang out she dealt with it very early, before her day's work began. In the evenings she went off to visit Liz Wells at the Lodge, or offered herself as babysitter to the Sewells. And when she did remain at home she occupied herself with paperwork and administration, just in case Alex sought her out. But she remained unsought. Which was just as well, she thought, lips tightening, one way or another.

The weather continued to be sunny and hot, and visitors swarmed to visit the house. The shop needed constant restocking of the expensive trifles that were popular as souvenirs, and the tea-shop was always full of thirsty customers grateful for tea and cakes, or cold drinks and ice-cream. A party of schoolchildren was shepherded round the building an hour before opening time one day, and there were usually people settled at various points, sketching the house and the Elizabethan stable block which housed the Sewells and Sarah and, for the time being, Alex Mackenzie.

Then one evening, as she was strolling back wearily towards the cottage at the end of her working day, Sarah found Alex waiting for her.

'Hello. You look tired,' he said with sympathy. 'Will you come in for a drink? I need your advice.'

Sarah was intrigued. 'How can I help you?'

Alex ushered her into his cool sitting-room. 'Let me get you a drink first. A glass of wine?'

'Thank you.'

Sarah sank into the corner of a sofa, yawning, only too happy to sit down. She smiled as Alex ducked back through the doorway, a frosted bottle in one hand, two glasses in the other.

'You're expert at low doorways now.'

He grinned as he poured then handed her a glass of wine. 'I've had one or two painful encounters *en route* to the kitchen, but I'm getting better.' He looked at her closely. 'You look exhausted. Full house again today?'

'Yes. Lots of people wanting lots of information. But I like it that way.' She raised an eyebrow at him. 'You said something about advice?'

Alex nodded. 'I mean help, actually. I'd like to have all the staff to an informal supper in the private quarters on Saturday. I wondered if you could arrange that for me—provide a caterer to do a cold meal, and so on? It's by way of thanks for all the help and co-operation I've been given while I've been here. I'll be off next week for a while—give Colonel Newby a chance to move his belongings out. Then I'll be back again by the middle of June with my bag and baggage.'

'I see.' Sarah drank a little of the dry, refreshing wine. 'Just give me some idea of the food you'd like. We use various caterers, depending on the type of refreshments wanted. If it's something small Liz Wells often does the food. She's a fantastic cook.'

'I'm sure she is, but since she's a guest let's make use of a professional caterer. I'll leave the menu to you—maybe seafood and ham, salads, that kind of thing. And some puddings.' He grinned. 'My taste doesn't run to those, but my father's does.'

'Your parents are coming, then?'

'They insisted when I told them what I had in mind. Couldn't keep them away.' Alex paused. 'How have you been, Sarah? I trust you're impressed by my exemplary behaviour?'

She smiled a little. 'I've been so busy I haven't noticed.'

'Now that,' said Alex, mock-tragic, 'is unkind. A man likes a woman to pay attention when he's being so unnaturally virtuous.'

'I'm sorry. I'll make a point of it from now on,' she assured him kindly.

Suddenly his attitude changed. 'Have you forgiven me?' he demanded abruptly.

She shrugged, making no pretence at misunderstanding. 'Just about.'

'I lost my temper completely—which is rare. It's an explanation, not an excuse.'

They looked at each other for a long moment, then Sarah said very quietly, 'I intend to forget the incident—put it out of my mind.'

'I'll try to do the same.' His mouth twisted in distaste. 'I would have reaffirmed my apology before this, but you've been damned elusive lately.'

As she'd intended. 'I've been busy.' Sarah finished her wine and got up. 'Thanks for the drink; I must dash. I'm bidden to the Sewells' barbecue.'

'I know. So am I.' He let out a bark of laughter at the look on her face. 'Are you about to be stricken with a sudden migraine and make excuses?'

It would be the sensible thing to do, Sarah knew. An evening spent in the starlight with Alex Mackenzie, even in the company of others, smacked of danger. She shook her head. 'I'm taking the salads. We do this often. Liz Wells makes a pudding and provides some of the meat, the Sewells do the rest. You, of course,' she added sweetly, 'being the boss, don't have to bring anything.'

'Lucky old me,' he murmured, and saw her to the door. 'I'll see you later, then. Can I help you carry anything?'

'I'd rather you didn't,' said Sarah bluntly. 'A lot of knowing looks came my way the day I had lunch with you. I've managed to put a stop to that. So I'd rather we arrived separately, please.'

'You haven't forgiven me, then.'

'That has nothing to do with it,' she retorted, then bit her lip. 'Well, maybe just a little. But, to be brutally honest, I really don't want my name coupled with yours, Alex. In any context.'

Alex's dark, slanting brows drew together. 'Whatever you wish, of course,' he said with chill courtesy.

'Thank you,' said Sarah in kind, and walked away along the brick path to her own front door, rather nettled to find that Alex, far from watching her go, had immediately retreated inside his own house and closed the door.

A couple of hours later, wearing white trousers and a filmy dark green shirt, her hair caught behind her ears with gilt combs, bare feet in gold thonged sandals, Sarah packed a large flat basket with dishes of salad, added a couple of jars of dressing, and tested the weight, wishing she'd let Alex carry it for her after all. As she opened the door to manoeuvre it out she found young Mr Henderson outside, looking stressed.

'Miss Law, I'm glad I caught you. We've just heard that my wife's mother has been rushed to hospital, so I'm afraid we'll have to cut our holiday short. We're driving north as soon as we get packed.'

'I'm so sorry; how worrying for you,' said Sarah with concern. 'Tell your wife to leave everything; don't bother to tidy up. Can I do something?'

'Not really.' He smiled ruefully. 'It's just that Emma knows something's up. She's holding up proceedings a bit.'

'Right,' said Sarah decisively. 'Just give me time to take this basket down to the Sewells, then I'll come back and look after Emma while you two get sorted out.'

'Oh, but—'

Sarah waved away his protests, shooed him back to his family, then hurried down to the Sewells' garden, handed the basket over to Janet, said she'd be back once the Hendersons were gone, and raced back to take charge of Emma. The baby's worried young mother handed her over with misgiving when she saw how Sarah was dressed.

'This is very good of you, but please be careful of your clothes, Miss Law.'

'They'll wash,' said Sarah, and received the sobbing baby with more confidence than she felt. 'I'll take her next door to my place—you knock when you're ready.'

Emma Henderson was incensed at being handed over to a stranger, and for a noisy few minutes Sarah had her work cut out to soothe the distressed baby. It seemed a long time before Emma decided she liked Sarah's perfume, and began to quieten a little as Sarah walked her up and down, singing all the nursery rhymes she could remember. Emma apparently liked the husky, off-key voice, and slowly relaxed against Sarah's shoulder, her small face hot and damp. She calmed down, hiccuping now and then with an errant sob, as Sarah paced slowly back and forth.

Alex appeared silently in the open doorway. 'I've been helping the Hendersons pack their car,' he whispered. 'How are you doing?'

'Fine,' Sarah mouthed at him. 'Are they nearly ready?'

He nodded. 'You can take the baby along now. Her mother's just making up a bottle for the journey.'

A few minutes later the worried young couple were on their way, with their daughter fast asleep in her car seat.

Sarah let out a long breath as the car disappeared up the lane. 'Poor things. What a shame their holiday was cut short—how did you know what was happening?'

'Janet Sewell told me, so I came back to see if I could give the poor guy a hand.' Alex smiled. 'But you were the real help. I wouldn't have the bottle to take charge of a baby.'

'I don't know that I had either,' said Sarah ruefully as she locked the empty cottage. 'To be honest I was terrified when Emma was handed over to me. She knew, too. But after a while we both settled down. I think she just wore herself out.'

'Nonsense. Pure expertise on your part,' he said firmly. 'Are you ready to come now? Or would you rather I went on ahead—or stayed behind?'

'Not much point now,' she said, shrugging. 'Give me a minute to tidy up. Miss Henderson was clutching at my hair. I thought she was going to pull it out by the roots at one stage—I must look a fright.'

'Far from it. The dishevelled look is ravishing,' he informed her, grinning. 'I'll smoke outside until you're ready.'

When they arrived at the Sewells' they were given much praise for their Good Samaritan act, handed glasses of wine, and told to relax. Sarah sank into the garden chair Jack Wells pulled forward next to his wife's, but Alex insisted on helping with the barbecue, surprisingly expert with the hamburgers and steaks.

'Quite a chap, our Mr Mackenzie,' murmured Liz in Sarah's ear. 'Rather a lad for the girls, I hear. Is he spoken for?'

'No idea,' said Sarah casually, and drank some of her wine. 'Probably.'

Liz nodded. 'That combination of confidence and tough good looks is pretty lethal. He's got charm, too. Do you like him?' she asked suddenly.

'Yes. I do. But that's as far as it goes,' said Sarah firmly.

Liz chuckled, recognising the hint, and told Jack they needed a refill.

'Great wine,' commented Sarah.

'Alex provided it,' said Jack. 'Brought it as his contribution.'

'A big improvement on the usual Sewell plonk,' said Tim as he came over to say that the meal was ready.

The evening was a great success from all points of view. Alex obviously enjoyed himself enormously as he wielded tongs over the coals, and eventually came to sit cross-legged on the grass near Liz and Sarah to eat his own meal, which, he said with mock modesty, was the best he'd ever tasted.

'Does it taste wonderful because I cooked some of it,' he asked, 'or because of the company and the surroundings?'

'A bit of both,' said Jack, munching contentedly.

Sarah was in full agreement. The meal was good, but the Sewells' barbecues were always good. It was the relaxed, happy mood everyone shared which made it special, and the fact that they were eating outdoors in the warmth of a perfect May evening, with the glow of sunset still lighting up the western sky. She saw Alex looking up at it and smiled.

'It rains and snows and gets cold here too, you know.'

'Are you trying to put me off?'

'No.'

'Good. Because once I make up my mind nothing changes it, Sarah,' he said in an undertone.

Sarah looked at him levelly, then jumped up. 'I'm going to help Liz with the puddings. You don't like sweet things, I know, but there's usually some cheese.'

Alex looked up at her challengingly. 'For once, maybe I'll change my mind. I'll have what you're having.'

Jack laughed, overhearing. 'Sarah always chooses the same thing—'

'Don't tell me what it is,' said Alex, grinning. 'Surprise me.'

Sarah stood over the embers of the dying coals, turning large bananas on the heat until the skins turned brown, then she hauled them off onto a platter for the others, put two aside onto plates, split them open, shook brown sugar and cinnamon onto the hot, soufflé-like fruit, while Liz added large scoops of her home-made vanilla ice-cream.

'Here you are,' said Sarah, handing Alex a plate as she sat down in her chair to enjoy the luscious flavours of the spicy fruit and the wickedly rich ice-cream.

Alex despatched his with shameless rapidity. 'Wonderful!' he said, chasing the last spoonful of ice-cream around his plate. 'If this is pudding I like it.'

Jack left them to fetch his own share, and for a moment Sarah and Alex were alone in their corner of the garden.

'Did you really like it, or were you just being polite?' said Sarah.

'I'm rarely polite when I feel otherwise,' he said sardonically. 'You experienced that first-hand, if you remember. I tend to say what I mean. I'm an uncomplicated sort of guy.'

Sarah snorted. 'Oh, come *on*!'

He laughed, and took her plate from her. 'No really. What you see is what you get—most of the time, anyway. I'll just take these back to Janet.'

The rest of the evening passed without any more private conversation, and Jack and Liz left earlier than usual.

'Got to walk her home before I get back to the house,' he said ruefully. 'I've kept on trying to persuade her to stay over there with me, but no luck.'

'No fear,' said Liz firmly. 'I don't mind lending a hand there in the daytime, but at night—no way.'

'You don't really think you'll see Ned Frome, do you?' asked Janet curiously.

'Since I'm never staying there overnight, no, I won't,' retorted Liz. 'Besides, Ned Frome apart, lots of people say there's a presence in the house—whoever, or whatever, it is.'

There was an odd little silence, then Jack laughed indulgently and put an arm round his wife. 'Come on, old girl, or you'll have me afraid of my own shadow.'

Janet and Tim Sewell insisted that Sarah and Alex stay for coffee.

'Don't desert us yet, or we'll get that awful flat, anticlimax feeling,' pleaded Janet. 'It's still early—the sky isn't even dark.'

It was very pleasant to sit in the now quiet garden, chatting companionably while they drank the coffee-pot dry.

'Such a luxury to be able to walk home,' said Alex, accepting a brandy. He leaned back in his chair, long legs stretched out as he looked up at the moon, which was almost full and lit up the garden like daylight. 'This is the most magical place.'

'We're all very lucky to live here,' said Tim with feeling. 'I was born only a few miles away, but I never imagined I'd one day be lucky enough to work at Ingham Lacey. I worked at big places like Penshurst and Hever Castle after college to gain experience, but to be head gardener at the house was always my dream.'

'Fortunate man,' said Alex quietly. 'Few people achieve such pleasure in their job.'

'I do,' said Sarah, and got up. 'Talking of which I must get back. I know the house is closed tomorrow, but that means all hands on deck with the floors. They were looking pretty scuffed this evening by locking-up time.'

After a friendly leave-taking, and graceful thanks for a very enjoyable evening, Alex walked with Sarah along the brick path past the dark cottage recently vacated by the Hendersons, and on past his own lamplit windows to Sarah's.

With every step Sarah grew more conscious of how solitary they were. The Sewells' part of the stable block was set at right angles to the other three, with the main rooms looking out onto their own small garden and the driveway leading from the main car park to the house. She shivered, glad of the sudden, eldritch screech of a hunting owl for providing a reason for it. Alex smiled as they halted outside her door.

'Surely you know an owl when you hear one!'

'Of course I do. But it's an eerie sound in the quiet, just the same.' Sarah put her key in the lock, then turned to him with a smile. 'You obviously enjoyed the evening. I hope the pudding doesn't give you indigestion.'

'Never suffer from it,' he assured her, grinning. 'In fact I seriously considered a second helping!'

Sarah laughed. 'Proof, as they say, of the pudding. Goodnight.'

'Goodnight.' He looked down at her steadily, then reached for her hand. 'Sarah, I don't want to say goodnight yet. If I swear to exemplary behaviour will you ask me in for a while?'

'If I say yes you'll misunderstand,' she said bluntly.

'All I'm asking is a little more time in your company, Sarah.'

She looked at him for a moment, then shrugged. 'All right. We'll have some coffee. But after that I really must call it a day. It's been a long one.'

'Which is my cue to behave like a gent and make myself scarce—but you offered coffee, so I'm staying!'

She laughed and opened the door, leading the way inside.

Alex followed Sarah through to the kitchen, and sat at the square oak table while she made the coffee. He looked around in approval. 'This is larger than I thought from the size of the other room.'

Sarah nodded. 'Should be the other way round, really, and yet not. I only sit to watch television, or read, in the parlour, whereas I use this as both office and kitchen.' She waved a hand at the computer on a small desk in the corner and the filing cabinet close by. 'Not your usual kitchen appliance, I know, but I like working here where I can look over the garden to the house—'

'Which you can't see from the other room, of course. You're totally in love with Ingham Lacey, aren't you?' broke in Alex as she brought a tray over to the table. 'Is there any room at all in your heart for anything—or anyone—else?'

'Of course there is,' she said tartly. 'I've got parents and a sister—and friends just like anyone else. I don't see them so much in the summer. It's a short season. Come October I'll be back in circulation, as usual.'

'I'm relieved,' he said drily as she filled the cups, then he frowned. 'Does that mean there's some man—or more than one—content to relinquish you for the summer until you've got time for him when it's over?'

Sarah sat down opposite him, cradling her cup in her hands. 'Unless they get themselves married in the meantime I've got a couple of contacts I look up in London. Sometimes one of them comes down here on a Saturday and takes me out for a meal. And now and then I have a couple of days off—even in summer—and go up to town for a session of bright lights and so on.'

'Good,' he said, pushing his empty cup aside. 'In that case what's to stop you wining and dining with me when you're next in town?'

'Prudence, caution, common sense—take your pick,' she said promptly.

Alex leaned back in his chair, his thumbs hooked through his belt loops. 'Why is it such a bad idea?'

'It isn't. But I won't just the same.'

'Why not? I don't think you dislike me. And to hark back to the other day you must admit that physically we're very compatible. In fact I want you like hell right this minute— No! Don't jump and hit me with a frying-pan. I promise I won't spoil things.' He smiled crookedly. 'It just seems such a waste.'

'A waste of what?' she demanded, stiffening.

'Of time, to start with. You are my precise idea of what a woman should be,' he said, startling her. 'Good-looking, but not obsessed with your looks, intelligent and efficient, but warm and compassionate too—as I saw with the baby tonight. But I've met a lot of women with all those qualities. You, Sarah, are alone in possessing that indefinable something which makes for this rapport between us.' He smiled into her eyes. 'Part of it is mental, the rest of it pure chemistry—as we discovered over lunch the other day.'

'I see,' said Sarah acidly, to cover the leap of her pulse. 'So you were actually teaching me a chemistry lesson, then.'

'I explained about that,' he said swiftly. 'I was carried away by the setting and the romance of the occasion, and all you could talk about was lust. I lost my temper. I could hardly spank you, so—'

'Please. We agreed to drop the subject. You were discussing waste originally, remember?'

'I was trying to explain that because we are two unattached people who find pleasure in each other's company it's a waste not to take advantage of the fact now and then,' he said reasonably. 'Surely no one at Ingham Lacey would find it strange if we went out for a meal together?'

Sarah laughed. 'Of course not! Some of the ladies would be ecstatic at the idea. The problem would lie in convincing them that we were just friends.'

'Would that matter to you?' Alex smiled triumphantly, sensing victory. 'It's your life. Surely you can run it the way you want, not the way others think you should?'

'Of course I do,' said Sarah impatiently, unwilling to let him know that it wasn't public opinion that was influencing her in the slightest, merely a deep-seated reluctance to lose the peace of mind which life at Ingham Lacey had achieved for her. Alex could wrap it up in whatever words he liked, but what he really wanted was an affair, rapport or no rapport. And getting over an affair with Alex Mackenzie might be a whole lot harder than getting over the debacle with Martin.

'So when can I take you out to dinner?' he demanded swiftly, and reached out to seize her hands. She looked down at the sinewy brown hands enfolding her own, feeling the roughness of his hard palms against hers, and wondered if any woman had ever said no to Alex Mackenzie in his life, other than his mother. 'I'll think about it,' she said, and he sat back, releasing her.

'You do damn all for my self-esteem, Sarah Law,' he said morosely.

'I've heard there's no lack of women willing to repair the damage,' she said, getting up.

'True,' said Alex simply, following suit. 'I enjoy the company of your sex, Sarah—but I'm not committed to anyone. Otherwise we wouldn't be having this conversation.' He smiled wryly. 'And you're the first to need time to think over a dinner invitation.'

'One strives for originality,' said Sarah drily. 'Now I really must say goodnight. I've got a lot to do tomorrow.'

Alex followed her to the door. 'I hope the party on Saturday isn't adding too much to your workload.'

'No, of course not. We have functions of some kind on Saturdays right through the summer.'

He bent to kiss her cheek, taking her by surprise. 'I'll probably see you before then, Sarah, but if not I shall expect you at eight on Saturday.'

'I'm afraid I need to be earlier than that,' she said, her pulse racing at the contact. 'Jack and I need to be on hand when anyone's in the house. These particular caterers are very reliable, but it's best to have someone around to supervise.'

'Then I'll make sure I get into my best bib and tucker nice and early,' he said, grinning. 'Goodnight, Sarah.' He looked down at her for a moment, hesitated, then pulled her into his arms and kissed her.

It was a long time before Alex raised his head, his eyes narrowed and glittering as they stared down into hers. 'Who knows when I'll be able to do that again? And I needed to. Goodnight. Sweet dreams.'

CHAPTER SIX

SARAH was up at the crack of dawn next day after a very restless night. Before the others had arrived she was in the house, ready to give a hand with the floors, which had to be completed before the midday zero hour.

'We can do this ourselves, Miss Law,' said one of the cleaners, deeply disapproving. 'No call for you to get yourself all hot and dirty, especially as it's only buffing today.'

Sarah, however, needed physical occupation. Traffic wax was used when the floors were actually polished, but in between they used wool cloths dampened with a mixture of paraffin and vinegar to repair the attentions of hundreds of feet as visitors made their way round the house. By ten it was all finished, and Sarah free to take a quick shower and tidy herself up before spending time on the phone to make sure that the caterers had no problems with the supper they were providing for Alex's party the following night.

By giving herself no time to think of anything other than matters concerning her job Sarah got through the day without too much introspection on the subject of Alex Mackenzie. She saw nothing of him during the day, and hurried back to her cottage when the house closed, going in by her kitchen door to avoid any possibility of encountering him. Tomorrow she had no choice about seeing him. Today she needed breathing space.

Sarah ate a swift, meagre supper, then took her portable television upstairs, leaving the ground floor in darkness so no one would disturb her.

She began to laugh once she was settled against her pillows. By no one, of course, she meant Alex. All this scuttling for cover was sheer cowardice. But Alex Mackenzie posed a powerful threat to her peaceful retreat at Ingham Lacey. Until his advent she'd been so impregnably serene and safe, sure that nothing would upset her equilibrium ever again, even smugly proud of the way she was on good terms with Martin and Isobel. Now one look from those silvery dark eyes of Alex Mackenzie, let alone one touch of his mouth on hers, and she was all to pieces.

Sarah sat up, suddenly erect, her eyes unseeing on the newscast she was watching. There was a solution to the problem, of course. If Alex came to live at Ingham Lacey, she would resign. It would mean staying until the end of the season; she couldn't let the team down by quitting before then. But Alex's idea of cosy little dinners now and then when he was in residence was out of the question, because... Because she was in love with the wretched man.

Sarah thrust her hands through her hair in despair. What a fool she was, deluding herself that she was in control, while all the time she was falling in love with Alex Mackenzie. And all he had in mind, it was perfectly obvious, were candlelit dinners and kisses—and bed, inevitably, too. And in this instance, for the first time since Martin, so did she. But she wanted them on a permanent basis. Like for life.

Sarah sagged back against the pillows, unaware that the news had given way to the latest instalment of the serial drama she liked. Her mouth twisted. At least she no longer needed time to think over his suggestion. In light of this new, daunting discovery the answer was most definitely no.

Next day Sarah spent an hour or two in the house in the morning, supervising the usual cleaning session, made sure that all was immaculate in the private quarters, ready for the evening, then told Jack she was out for the afternoon.

'Good. Going somewhere nice?'

'Tunbridge Wells, shopping,' said Sarah. 'The caterers aren't due until six. I'll be back well before then.'

'Right. Don't worry. I'll be around. Enjoy yourself—and drive carefully,' he said affectionately.

'Careful is my middle name, Jack. See you later.'

As Sarah crossed the narrow lane to the small private car park in the field Alex emerged from his cottage.

'How are you today?' he asked, crossing the lane. 'I was up in London all day yesterday, didn't get back until late. Everything in train for tonight?'

So the frightened rabbit act had been unnecessary after all. Sarah's smile was cool, her secret annoyance battling with the rush of pleasure she felt at the sight of him. 'Of course. The caterers arrive at six. I'll be back before then.'

'Where are you going?' he demanded. 'Will you be long?'

'No idea. Don't worry. I'll be on hand when I'm needed!'

His eyes lit with an unholy gleam. 'Then stay for a moment. I haven't laid eyes on you for thirty-six hours. Did you know the midday sun sets your hair on fire?'

This wasn't fair.

'I can certainly feel it frying my brains,' said Sarah prosaically. 'So I'd better be off. See you later.' With a casual wave of her hand she got in her car and opened the sun roof, very conscious that Alex remained where he was, watching her out of sight as she drove recklessly fast up the narrow lane to get herself away from the eyes which quite plainly told her he was remembering how they'd parted in the moonlight. They told her even more plainly that he wanted to make love to her again right now, in the bright, hot light of day.

The trip to Tunbridge Wells was no mere escape from the delights and dangers of Ingham Lacey for a few hours. Sarah needed something new to wear to the party. She wanted to look her best when she told Alex Mackenzie she was declining the offer of becoming his lover. Pity. Perhaps if they weren't based at Ingham Lacey, but had met in the usual way in London, each with a flat of their own to provide privacy for a love affair—but no! Not even then, Sarah told herself savagely. Love affairs were designed to self-destruct. A long, long period of post-affair misery was too high a price to pay for a few days, weeks, even months of what might not, after all, be unalloyed bliss, even with Alex. Her experience with Martin had taught her that.

Sarah returned to her cottage out of pocket, but certain that tonight she would look as good as it was possible to look. A phone call the day before had cajoled an appointment from the man who trimmed her hair from time to time, and now it gleamed with professional lustre, an inch or two shorter, its slight natural wave enhanced with a skill which had been expensive, but worth it, Sarah decided, after she'd taken a bath tepid enough to prevent steam damage on the finished result.

The dress she'd bought had been reduced in price because, the sales assistant had told her, the colour was difficult for most people to wear, and didn't sell well in summer. The dark, bitter chocolate shade drained some types of colouring, but on Sarah it emphasised her creamy skin and exactly matched her eyes. The dress was a starkly plain tube of raw silk, sleeveless, high-necked, and shorter than she normally wore. The sales girl's patter had been superfluous. Sarah had known the dress was hers the moment it slid into place over her hips.

She highlighted her eyes more than usual, using darker shadow in the hollows and ivory on the lids to emphasise the dreamy look which had first caught Alex's attention. Two coats of dark mascara, careful application of russet lipstick, amber drop pendants from her ears and Sarah was ready to take on the world, Alex Mackenzie included.

As the clock in the tower struck six Sarah locked her cottage and strolled down the path bordering the lawn, her heels clicking on the wooden boards of the draw-bridge as she crossed the moat. As Sarah climbed the stone stairs to the private apartments she heard a van coming down the drive from the public car park and smiled with satisfaction. The caterers were on time, and so was she. There would be no opportunity for private conversation with Alex.

Sarah was right. When the door opened to her knock Alex stood stock-still, transfixed at the sight of her, the look on his face sufficient reward for the trouble she'd taken.

'Lord,' he said reverently, and breathed in deeply. 'You look—breathtaking. Come in.'

'Don't keep the lady on the doorstep,' said an amused voice, and a man appeared at Alex's shoulder, not nearly as tall, slim and erect, with sandy hair and bright blue eyes. A man she'd noticed often enough among the visitors to Ingham Lacey.

'You, I know, are Miss Sarah Law,' he said, holding out his hand. 'I'm Alexander Mackenzie. We've seen each other before.'

'How do you do?' said Sarah, smiling. 'We have indeed. No one ever told me who you were.'

'I prefer to remain anonymous! Come in, my dear, and meet my wife. Alex, I think the caterers are arriving.'

'Right,' said Alex, tearing his eyes away from Sarah with gratifying reluctance. 'I'll go and let them in.'

Alexander Mackenzie led Sarah into the drawing-room, where a woman was lying on a sofa, reading. She got to her feet with a smile, thrusting them into the small kid sandals she had obviously just kicked off. She wore a blue dress as plain as Sarah's, and her greying blonde hair was cut in a casual windswept style, emphasising the youthfulness of an attractive, tanned face which was instantly familiar.

'Miss Law, how nice to meet you officially at last. I've seen you often, of course.' She held out her hand, smiling warmly. 'You do a terrific job here.'

'Thank you.' Sarah took the hand, liking Alex's mother on sight. 'I've noticed you both before, often. But I would never have placed you as Alex's parents— you both look too young.' Neither was there any resemblance to their son.

'You've made a friend for life!' laughed Alexander Mackenzie. 'Ellen caught me young, Miss Law; we met in our first year at college.'

'Sandy tells everyone he was a child bride,' said his wife, resigned. 'We did marry unfashionably young by today's standards, it's true—straight after our finals.' She looked up as her tall, dark son came into the room, looking more attractive than a man had a right to, in Sarah's opinion, in a pale linen suit of unmistakable Italian cut.

Alex smiled wryly. 'It's a handicap having parents who look more like my siblings than the actual siblings. Sorry to break it up, but the caterers are demanding your presence, Sarah.'

'Right. I'll just make sure it's the usual team.'

'Come back quickly and have a glass of champagne,' said Sandy Mackenzie. 'Let the others do the work tonight, Sarah. I may call you Sarah?'

'Of course.' Sarah smiled her thanks and went from the room and along the hall to the kitchen, where the caterers were busy unpacking the meal. She spoke to the efficient young woman in charge, who'd been to Ingham Lacey many times before and was well used to the routine. Sarah made sure the dining-room was in readiness, checked that the leather protective cover was under the starched white damask cloth on the table, then went back to the drawing-room, where Alex was alone, standing at the window. He turned as Sarah went in.

'Come and join me in a drink. Mother's gone to do something to her face, and Dad's just having a chat with Jack Wells in the courtyard.'

Sarah took the glass of champagne he poured for her, then stood with him at the window, watching Tim Sewell watering the flowerbeds.

'You look breathtaking tonight,' said Alex quietly. 'My parents are deeply impressed.'

'How nice of them. They were a surprise. I know their faces well enough, of course, as I do many of the regulars, but I expected your father to be an older version of you.'

Alex grinned. 'I'm the dead spit of old Alex, my grandfather. Dad takes after his mother.'

'Were you the apple of your grandfather's eye, by any chance?' she queried, smiling.

'In his own gruff kind of way, yes.' Alex shrugged. 'Which made him harder on me than anyone else. My sisters follow my mother for looks. I'm unadulterated Mackenzie, which is a two-edged sword. It meant that old Alex made sure I came up through the firm the hard way. It didn't do me any harm, though I could have done without the fights along the way to prove I was no namby-pamby daddy's boy—witness the dent in my nose! But sometimes I get restless, wish I wasn't the heir apparent, as you keep putting it. I know I'll be in charge some day, of course, but now you've met my father it's easy to see it won't be yet awhile. Dad's only fifty-four, in perfect health and still full of enthusiasm for the job. He won't abdicate his throne for years—nor do I want him to.'

'Do you mean you'd have liked to do something else?' asked Sarah.

'Promise not to laugh?'

'Yes.'

'I wanted to paint. You know the kind of thing—starve in a garret, the bohemian life, and all that.' Alex pulled a face. 'Old Alex laughed the idea out of court.'

Sarah eyed him curiously. 'What did your father think of the idea?'

'He was all for it if I was really set on it. But he made it very clear that if I did that, after spending years training to be an architect, I had to make it on my own, with no financial assistance.'

'Which damped your ardour.'

'Not a bit of it. I was all set to leave when old Alex had a stroke. I think he did it on purpose,' added Alex drily. 'He couldn't walk, lost the use of one arm, but he could still talk, the old devil. Pulled out every stop in the book to persuade me to change my mind. So in the end I did.'

'You were fond of him,' said Sarah quietly.

'I was. But I was even fonder of my grandmother.' Alex smiled wryly. 'She was the one who coaxed me to stay a while, wait until he was better. Or dead. Not one for mincing her words, Joan Mackenzie.'

'Did he get better?'

'No. But he didn't die either. At least not for quite a while. And by then I was part of the firm, surprised to find myself interested in most of the work, especially on the conservation side. My dreams of being the next Hockney, or Jackson Pollock, began to fade.' He touched her bare arm very lightly with the tip of one finger, trailing it down to her wrist. 'But I do dabble occasionally. I go on holiday to Provence and Umbria, and to the Glens, of course.'

'I'd like to see some of your work,' said Sarah, trying to ignore the feather-light touch, half expecting to see a burn on her skin when he moved away as his parents' voices sounded in the hall.

'If I asked you up here to see my sketches,' he muttered, 'I can imagine your response!'

She giggled involuntarily, and Alex threw open the window to lean out.

'Hey, Tim,' he shouted through cupped hands. 'Get a move on. It's nearly party time.'

The Mackenzies, all three of them, were very good hosts. Everyone present, including the various partners of the actual employees, was given a warm welcome and pressed to partake of all the delicacies provided. The numbers involved meant the rooms of the private quarters were comfortably crowded, with no opportunity for the shyest person present to feel left out as Alex and his parents circulated, with Sarah on hand to make any necessary introductions. Everyone warmed to Ellen Mackenzie's genuine friendliness, as she asked after families, and even produced photographs of her own grandchildren to pass round.

'My sisters' hellions,' Alex informed Sarah.

'Time *you* provided me with a few, too,' said his mother, overhearing.

Alex bolted, muttering something about drinks.

'Really!' said Ellen irritably. 'Alex is impossible. The merest mention of settling down or getting married and he's off like a greyhound. He's thirty-three, you know. By that age we had three children.'

Sandy Mackenzie shook his head at his wife. 'Leave Alex alone, Ellie. No trespassing in that area. We were an exception. People don't get married young these days.'

Sarah, feeling a little embarrassed, excused herself, but Ellen Mackenzie put a hand on her arm. 'Stay and talk to me for a while. Sandy can circulate. I need a sit down.'

'You will wear those silly shoes!' said her husband affectionately, and went off to join his son, leaving the two women together on a window seat.

'You're quite young for this job, Sarah,' said Ellen. 'It's a big responsibility.'

'Ingham Lacey is relatively small. Otherwise the job would have gone to someone older, with more experience.'

'I fancy it couldn't have gone to anyone who loved the place more.'

'Thank you. That's a very kind thing to say.'

'But the truth.' Ellen smiled mischievously. 'I purposely didn't tell Alex you were so young, Sarah. You came as quite a surprise.'

Sarah chuckled. 'Oh, yes. He was expecting Mrs Danvers, I think, black dress and keys included. I do have a bunch of keys, but I'm afraid I work in jeans when the house is closed.'

'Mrs Wells was full of praise for you, Sarah. I gather you do far more hands-on work yourself than the former housekeeper.'

'I enjoy it. And it gives me a good idea of the time and energy necessary to do each job properly. And some things only I can do anyway, because I was trained for them—like taking care of the more valuable ceramic pieces.'

Curious blue eyes scanned Sarah's face. 'But don't you have some young man chafing somewhere at playing second fiddle to this place?'

'No. I see some friends when I go up to my sister in London, or to my parents in Gloucestershire. But during the summer season we're very busy here. I tend to stay put except for the odd day off now and again.'

Ellen shook her head. 'A sequestered sort of life for a beautiful girl like you.'

'But one I like very much,' said Sarah, then could have kicked herself, remembering her intention to resign. What reason was she going to give? 'Can't stay because Alex Mackenzie's coming to live here' wasn't the sort of thing one put in a letter of resignation.

'Come on, you two,' said Alex, coming to interrupt. 'The pudding course has arrived on the table, and you know you're a glutton for sweet things, Mother, dear.'

Ellen, whose figure was rounded but very trim, gave her son a glare. 'Are you saying I'm overweight, Alexander Mackenzie?'

'Would I dare?' he said wryly, and grinned at Sarah. 'I only get my full name when she's angry.'

'Which isn't often,' said his mother, and linked her arm through his. 'Come on, Sarah, let's treat ourselves to something sinful.'

The party was a big success. The private quarters of the house were rarely used for functions, and the locals who'd never been inside them before obviously felt privileged to be there. The festivities continued until a little after midnight, when Janet and Tim Sewell took their leave, beginning a slow exodus of guests, everyone thanking Alex for a wonderful evening as he showed them out.

His parents were returning to London that night, to Sarah's surprise.

'Don't worry, dear, our driver's waiting in the car park.' Ellen smiled, taking Sarah's hand. 'Everything went like a dream tonight, thanks to you.'

'It was the caterers, really!'

'But in an unobtrusive way you were everywhere, making sure that everyone had a good time and the caterers were doing their job.' Ellen squeezed her hand. 'We'll meet again.'

'Next time you come to a concert I'll save you the best seat,' promised Sarah, smiling.

'I hope I'll see you before then, now Alex is going to live here—don't look at me like that, Sandy! I shan't be running down here every five minutes.'

Her husband laughed. 'Alex is a grown man, Ellie. He can look after himself.'

'Hmm.' Ellen looked unconvinced.

Alex came to say that the driver had brought the car down to the main gates and everyone else had left.

'Thanks, Alex,' said his father, shaking his hand. 'Great party—good public relations. Always wise to get to know your staff.'

'Come on, Sandy,' urged his wife. 'Alex tells me Sarah has to check over the rooms before she can leave, to make sure nothing's missing.'

'Then it's time we were off!' Sandy Mackenzie shook Sarah's hand. 'You do a great job here, Sarah. Everyone I spoke to had nothing but praise for you.'

'Thank you.'

'Sarah, I'll just see my parents off the premises, then I'll come back to give you a hand,' said Alex.

'Are you going to search us before we go?' asked his mother, waving at Sarah as she left.

Sarah heard Alex laughing in the hall, then the sound of the front door closing, and went to the desk in the office to take out the inventory. It would have been unnecessary in the rest of the building, but here in the private quarters she was less familiar with the contents.

She was in the dining-room, checking pieces of silver against the list, when Alex came back.

'Nothing missing, I hope?' he asked.

'Not so far.' She handed him the inventory. 'You read out the items, I'll check they're all present and correct.'

It took very little time to reassure Sarah that everything was in its place, including the bedrooms, where the walls were hung with some valuable Victorian watercolours.

'Right,' she said at last, smiling at him. 'All done.'

'Good,' said Alex. 'Now we are alone and in no danger of being either seen or overheard, I want to say how much I appreciate the way you organised the evening. You were a big hit with my parents. Thank you, Sarah.' He reached into his coat pocket and brought out a small, flat parcel. 'I'd like you to have this as a small token of my appreciation.'

Sarah took the parcel with misgiving. 'I don't need a present.'

'Open it!' he ordered. 'It's nothing valuable, I promise. In fact you'll probably laugh.'

She took off the wrappings to reveal a miniature, giltframed oil painting. Her eyes narrowed for a moment, then opened wide in astonishment. The subject was a head and shoulders study of an angel, very Pre-Raphaelite in style, in a dark green robe, with long red hair flowing down between two, just visible wing-tips. It could have been a detail from a work by Millais at first glance, but for one important feature. Sarah stared in astonishment at the dreaming, heavy-lidded profile standing out in relief against a grey stone background.

'It's me!' she said, amazed. 'How—?'

'My work entirely,' said Alex, sounding, for once, oddly diffident.

'But it's exquisite! Not me, I mean,' she added hastily. 'The painting itself.' She took it to a lamp and propped it beneath the light to study it. 'When did you do it?'

'I had the idea the moment I first saw you.' He came close behind her to look down at the small painting. 'That was my first glimpse of you at the concert—minus the wings, of course. When I found I was to be in day-to-day contact with you I thought I'd put my spare time at the cottage to good use. Do you like it?'

'Of course I like it. It's quite wonderful!' Sarah turned impulsively to kiss him on the cheek, and Alex caught her in his arms and kissed her mouth with sudden, hungry need.

'How I've got through the evening without doing that I'll never know,' he said hoarsely into her hair.

It was the last time this would ever be possible, Sarah told herself, surrendering abruptly to a mixture of emotions, one of which was overwhelming curiosity. She so badly needed to know what love would be like with Alex. Love, not lust, she reminded herself with something like a sob as Alex kissed her with a tenderness so unlike his brief, brutal lesson beside the stream that she melted into his arms, returning his kisses with a fervour which vanquished Alex's self-control.

He shrugged out of his jacket and pulled his tie away, then drew her down on the sofa until they lay full-length together. 'Sarah, don't keep me at arm's length.'

Since they were lying so close together that they could hardly breathe, Sarah laughed breathlessly. 'This is arm's length?'

Alex drew in a long, unsteady breath, crushing her close. 'I want you so much. It was hell to stay polite for the last half-hour tonight. I was willing everyone to go, to leave me alone with you so I could do this...and this...' He felt her tremble in response to his touch and kissed her until her head reeled. He lifted his head at last to look down into her dazed, dreaming eyes. 'Stay with me tonight.'

CHAPTER SEVEN

SARAH answered him without words. Just this one night, she told herself, in an attempt to placate the warning voice in her mind, and felt him shudder in response to her caressing hands. Her body curved against him in exultation as she discovered the havoc she was creating with Alex's self-control, and she held him close, not caring that his arms threatened to break her ribs. She felt his heart thundering against hers and luxuriated in the storm she was rousing in the hard, muscular body, so different from anything she'd known with Martin.

Alex sat up abruptly and tore off his shirt, and she slid her hands slowly over his broad chest. She smiled into his eyes as they dilated, his muscles tensing under her caress, her fingers feather-light as they moved along his collarbone and up to travel over his shoulders until she locked them behind his neck, bringing his head down to hers. Their lips met with fierce hunger, and Alex pulled her down with him again full-length, one hand running down her spine to hold her so close that every part of his body seemed imprinted in fire on her own. She opened her eyes to see the glitter of desire in his and pushed him away so that she could stand up.

'Where are you going?' he demanded hoarsely, leaping up.

'Nowhere!' She kicked off her shoes and reached behind her for the zip of her dress, letting the silk slither slowly to her feet. She stepped out of it then turned to him, holding out her arms.

Alex drew in a sharp, unsteady breath, then snatched her up and carried her swiftly to the master bedroom. 'I can't believe this is happening,' he said unevenly as he laid her down. He hung over her, his eyes dark with need as they took in every curve and hollow of her body. 'Is this a dream, Sarah?'

She held up her arms. 'I'm flesh and blood, if that's what you mean. Touch me and see.'

Alex let himself down beside her, turning her so that she lay against him, her face against his throat. He ran his hands over her hips, his mouth meeting hers as she turned it up to him in invitation. Engulfing kisses removed every last restraint as hands and lips caressed each other in mounting frenzy, until Sarah made a choked little sound of protest, feeling cold and bereft when Alex leapt from the bed. She lay with an arm over her eyes, heart beating so loudly that she barely registered the slight sounds as he shed the last of his clothes.

She heard the bed creak as he came down beside her, feeling the night air cold on her skin as her silk underwear was peeled away from her body, then heat and wonderful, breathtaking contact as their bodies touched and flowed against each other, hard muscles and angles fitting into curves and hollows with ravishing precision. Alex said wild, gratifying things in her ear, his voice so hoarse with feeling that she shivered and clutched him closer, as much on fire as he. They kissed and caressed each other to a point of mutual arousal so intense that neither could bear to be separate a second longer, their bodies uniting with such rhythmic implacability that their desire

rapidly to heights which they scaled, reaching
of rapture far beyond Sarah's imaginings.

first acquaintance with fulfilment was over-
ming, almost unbearable in its brief, throbbing in-
tensity, before aftermath overtook them, as pleasurable
in its own way as the rapture which preceded it.

They lay bathed in the light of the setting moon, silent
in each other's arms, held fast in a spell of enchantment
which held them motionless until at last desire ignited
again, to Sarah's astonishment, and Alex began to make
love to her once more. This time he was very much in
control, and lingered over every teasing touch and caress,
his kisses even more erotic in their slow enticement as
he coaxed her gradually and inexorably on the path they
had rushed along before. It took a long, long time—so
long that when they were quiet at last in each other's
arms Alex fell deeply asleep almost at once, his head
against her shoulder.

Sarah lay motionless for over an hour, listening to his
deep, even breathing, her cheek against the crisp, curling
hair, as she allowed herself this last, never-to-be-repeated
luxury. Her heart, which had beaten so fast to the rhythm
of their lovemaking, began to ache at the thought of
what came next. She moved little by little from his arms,
lying still for a moment when he stirred and muttered
as his head found the pillow instead of her shoulder.
After a while he sank back into deep sleep, and Sarah
slid from the bed, picked up the garments Alex had
tossed aside, and stole from the room.

The moon had set, and two dim security lights at either
end of the house were the only glow in the starlit
darkness. In the sitting-room Sarah put on her clothes
hurriedly without a light, collected her shoes and bag

and the painting Alex had given her, then went from the private quarters without making a sound, leaving by the kitchen entrance.

Feeling like a thief in the night, Sarah crept over the small bridge across the moat at the back of the house, out of sight of the stable cottages. She made a deliberate detour past the shop and the restaurant, skirting the Italian garden to take the path along the wilderness walk to avoid the battery of security lights which would flood on if she went directly from the house across the lawn. Sarah was so intent on getting home unseen that she hardly noticed the rustlings and night sounds of the woodland gardens, where she'd never ventured after dark before.

Stumbling once or twice, tripping in the darkness over unseen obstacles, she finally reached the side-gate of her own little garden, and let herself in by the kitchen door, suddenly so tired that it was all she could do to get herself upstairs and creep into bed, so overcome with weariness that she immediately sank into a sleep as deep as Alex's.

Morning came mercilessly early, overcast and humid, and brought with it Sarah's bitter regret for having yielded to temptation the night before. Nothing, not even the bliss experienced in Alex Mackenzie's arms, was worth this feeling of utter desolation.

Her eyes felt hot and dry as she lay in the bath, and her mood was black as she dressed in a white shirt and slim navy linen skirt, brushed her hair up into a cruelly tight knot, then went downstairs to make herself some breakfast. She drank several cups of tea, but found it quite impossible to eat. She gave up at last, and washed up out of habit, then dodged out of sight suddenly as she saw Alex walking across the lawn. Her heart gave a sickening thump as she saw him hesitate, eyeing her window. He fingered the villainous black stubble on his chin, obviously thinking better of the idea, and turned away to his own cottage.

Sarah hurried upstairs for her keys, slapped some make-up on her pallid face, groaned at the dark circles under her eyes, and went down in a hurry to escape before Alex came looking for her. After last night he might well think he had no need to be discreet any more. Nor, she thought bitterly, could she blame him. Her cheeks burned at the memory of her abandon. Martin had always accused her of immature prudery. How astonished he would be if he knew. But no more than she was.

Alex, of course, was a consummate lover. He'd proved that beyond all doubt the second time, if not the first. With Martin she'd faked the ultimate pleasure. With Alex it had been so different that her heart thumped painfully now at the mere thought of it. But such expertise made it painfully obvious that he'd had a great deal of practice. And she had no intention of providing him with any more. Even without the reputation that preceded him, his mother's words were confirmation enough. No matter how good they were together, in bed or out of it, sooner or later Alex would take off for pastures new. And no way was she laying herself open to that a second time.

Sarah left her cottage by the back door, taking something of the same roundabout route she'd followed in darkness in the night, just in case Alex might be watching from his window. She gained the house without detection, it being far too early for anyone else to be about, and made straight for the private quarters. Most people knew that Alex had taken Jack's place there for the night, but with luck, and care, no one would need know that Sarah Law had spent the major part of the night there too.

Sarah quickly stripped the bed where Alex had taught her how little she'd known before about love. Her cheeks burned at the chaotic state of it. Nothing of his remained, other than the scent of him mingled with her own, which drifted up as she folded the silky tangled linen. Sarah swallowed hard and forced herself to carry on, and as she bundled everything into a laundry bag she caught sight of something shining on the carpet. Her earring! Sarah went on her hands and knees, searching frantically for the other amber drop, but without success.

Sarah left the laundry in the kitchen for collection and went to the drawing-room. The wrappings from her picture were still on a side-table, and the cushions on the bigger sofa were deeply indented where she'd lain with Alex. She plumped up the cushions viciously, slapping them into place. She made a thorough search for her missing earring, gave it up at last as hopeless, collected the wrapping paper and went down into the main house, where Jack Wells was just arriving.

'Good morning, Sarah,' he said in surprise. 'You're an early bird.'

'I saw Alex leave the flat, so I thought I'd better get over here and do some superficial tidying before the cleaning team move in to put everything straight for Colonel Newby. He's back tomorrow.' Sarah smiled brightly. 'Great party, wasn't it?'

He nodded, eyeing her with concern. 'You look like the morning after the night before, Sarah.'

How right he was. 'Two glasses of champagne,' she said lightly. 'One glass too many.'

Jack looked unconvinced. 'Just the same you don't look too clever. If you feel rough just say the word; the rest of us can cope.'

'Thank you, I will.' But she had no intention of keeping the promise. The last thing she wanted was a day on her own at the cottage with time to think. Better by far to keep occupied at the house—out of Alex's way.

Sarah achieved this until just before one, when Jack found her in the chapel, talking to a group of visitors.

'Miss Law, Mr Mackenzie would like a word with you,' he said formally, and she excused herself and left the chapel with him.

'Did he say what he wanted?' she asked, wanting quite desperately to run away and hide.

'Apparently he's leaving shortly. He's waiting in the cottage. See you later.'

Alex's door stood open, but when she knocked he came swiftly to draw her down into the sitting-room, shutting the door behind her.

'You've been avoiding me,' he accused, grasping her hands. He frowned in concern as he looked down into her face. 'You look fragile, Sarah. Headache?'

'No, just lack of sleep,' she said rashly, then bit her lip.

He smiled. 'I slept like the dead until seven or so. I suppose you left long before then.'

'Yes.'

Alex pulled on her hands with the obvious intention of kissing her, but Sarah resisted and his eyes narrowed.

'Regrets?'

'Not really.' Sarah's eyes met his unflinchingly. 'I was an equal partner in what happened last night. But—'

'Does there have to be a but?'

'I hope you'll believe that the episode was out of character for me.'

Alex smiled indulgently. 'I knew that right from the start.'

Sarah frowned. 'How?'

His grasp tightened. 'It was obvious, Sarah. The entire experience was sheer perfection for me from the moment I took you in my arms, not least because you were so ravishingly inexpert—'

'Inexpert?'

He nodded emphatically, his eyes relentless as they challenged hers. 'Admit it, Sarah. Until last night, the amorous professor or not, you'd never achieved—'

'Please!' she said imperiously. 'In-depth analysis of my sexual experience—or lack of it—is rather distasteful in the cold light of day.' She detached her hands firmly. 'Jack said you're leaving, and that you wanted to see me.'

Alex stepped back, frowning. 'Yes, on both counts. My father wants me in Frankfurt at the crack of dawn tomorrow, so I'm flying over this afternoon, which answers the first part. And naturally I wanted to see you. Did you expect me to post my keys through your letterbox and take off without a word?'

'No,' she said, her eyes falling.

'But you'd have preferred it that way, obviously.' He moved to the desk and picked up the keys, holding them out to her. 'There you are, then, Miss Law. If you look over the cottage you'll find everything in place, nothing broken or missing.'

Sarah took the keys from him with polite thanks.

Alex regarded her in brooding silence. 'Like a fool,' he said, after a tense interval, 'I thought that last night was a beginning. It seems I was mistaken.'

She nodded. 'I'm afraid so. You talked about friendship, but you really meant a relationship based on what happened last night.'

'I suppose, in my heart of hearts, I did, yes,' he admitted bleakly. 'I'm a normal sort of guy. I think we could share something very special together. A meeting of minds as well as the physical part. Which from my point of view was sublime. But—' he shrugged, his eyes hard '—if you don't agree I'm not the type to beg. Life's too short.'

'And the world, as it always has been for you, full of other women.'

Alex shrugged carelessly. 'Quite so. Goodbye for now, Sarah. Thank you for arranging the party last night.'

'Thank you for the gift,' she returned equably. 'Though perhaps you'd like me to return it.'

'Keep it as a souvenir.' His eyes were bitter. 'Though I was wrong to portray you as an angel. Only a devil would have allowed last night to happen and then tell me to get lost next morning.'

Her eyebrows rose. 'Allowed?'

'At any time last night all you had to say was no. But— correct me if I'm wrong, of course—you seemed to want me as much as I wanted you.' He flung up a hand like a fencer. 'Don't worry—you're in no danger. What I'm trying to say is that if I'd known last night was to be a one-off, Sarah, I wouldn't have touched you.'

'I'm sorry you were misled.'

'That makes two of us!' Alex strode to the door. He turned to her, his eyes sardonic. 'Isn't there a quotation somewhere—"'Tis better to have loved and lost/Than never to have loved at all"?'

'Tennyson,' she said through stiff lips.

'The man was talking through his hat!' He inclined his head formally. 'Goodbye, Sarah.'

When Alex had gone Sarah sat down at her computer, wrote a brief letter of resignation and put it aside to give to Colonel Newby when he arrived next day. Not, she thought, depressed, the best way to greet him on his return, even if she was offering to stick it out throughout the summer until he found a replacement.

It would be painful with Alex in residence part of the time. But there was no alternative. It wasn't the kind of post one could fill at a moment's notice. The former housekeeper had stayed on for several weeks to ensure the smooth running of the house when it was given over into such youthful hands. But that was over three years ago. Now, for one reason and another, thought Sarah wearily, she felt older and sadder but not appreciably wiser. A fortnight of knowing Alex Mackenzie would be far more difficult to get over than the time she'd wasted waiting for Martin Dryden to marry her.

Colonel Newby was a brisk, burly man with a bluff exterior which belied his inner kindness. Sarah took very little pleasure in handing him her resignation next day.

'But why, Sarah?' he asked, mystified. 'We all thought you were so happy here.'

'I know. And I have been. But it's time I made a move.'

He shook his head. 'I arrived back in a state of euphoria when I heard the consortium had no changes in mind and that young Alex Mackenzie was moving into the house. I thought there had to be *some* fly in the ointment.' He smiled ruefully. 'I didn't dream it would be you, Sarah.'

'I'm perfectly willing to stay for the summer while you look for a replacement,' she said guiltily. 'I'll have time to look for another post, too.'

The Colonel stared at her aghast. 'Are you telling me you don't have another job to go to, Sarah?'

Her eyes fell. 'Yes. It was rather a sudden decision.'

'I see. Or rather I don't.' He shook his head as she got up to go. 'Perhaps we'll manage to change your mind before you burn your boats, Sarah. In the meantime, of course, I'm obliged to pass your resignation on to the consortium.'

'Of course.' Sarah sighed ruefully. 'Sorry to spring this on you on your first day back. How is Mrs Newby?'

'As usual all the better for a break in the sun. She's very relieved by the solution to the problem, by the way.' He grimaced. 'Told me she didn't fancy having me under her feet at home all day for a few years yet.'

Sarah chuckled. 'My mother felt the same when my father retired. Now she complains he's found so much to do that she sees less of him than ever.'

'Contrary lot, you ladies.' He looked her straight in the eye. 'I could have sworn you were an exception, Sarah.'

CHAPTER EIGHT

ONCE Sarah's resignation was common knowledge life became difficult. She told Jack and Liz Wells and the Sewells personally, before it was made public to the rest of the staff, and found their horrified reaction very gratifying in one way, but very hard to take in others. Mainly because she felt so guilty. Not that she had any choice now that Alex Mackenzie was coming to live at Ingham Lacey, Sarah told herself flatly.

But now and again her certainty wavered. The reason she gave everyone for her resignation was the need for change, before she took root at Ingham Lacey and stayed there until her retirement. She could hardly tell them she was afraid of giving in to temptation where Alex was concerned, with everyone at Ingham Lacey as onlookers while the affair ran its course. And inevitably ended. No way could she endure that.

'I'm in danger of becoming a fixture,' she said lightly, but Liz Wells looked at her with sharp eyes, experience with her own daughters telling her that Sarah's private reason was very different from the official version.

In the time before Alex moved in, Mrs Newby's sister arrived to keep her company so that the Colonel could sleep in the private quarters. For the entire fortnight Alex's imminent arrival hung over Sarah like the sword of Damocles. Their parting had been difficult enough to make their next meeting awkward in the extreme. But when Alex Mackenzie finally arrived on the appointed

107

day, when the house was closed to the public, awkward was too lukewarm a word by far to describe their first encounter.

Sarah was casting an eye over the private quarters to see that all had been left spick and span for Alex's arrival when she heard his voice on the stairs before she had time to escape. He stopped on the threshold of the sitting-room, and dumped down a pair of suitcases at the sight of Sarah.

'Good afternoon,' she said quietly. 'We weren't expecting you quite so early.'

His arrogant smile did nothing to put her at ease. 'Why, Miss Law, complete with keys and inventory. How nice of you to act as a welcoming committee.'

Colonel Newby, following behind with a large grip, smiled warmly. 'Just checking I left everything in order, Sarah?' He turned to beckon someone else into the room. 'Come in, my dear. Let me introduce you to Sarah Law, the housekeeper at Ingham Lacey.'

A slender girl in skin-tight jeans and clinging scarlet vest strolled into the room, pushing back a waterfall of blonde hair from her face. 'How do you do?' she said in surprise. 'Goodness, I thought—'

'The housekeeper would be older,' said Alex sardonically. 'It's one of the mistakes people make with Sarah. Her looks are misleading. She's really Mrs Danvers in disguise.'

'Don't be so rude!' said the girl, and held out her hand to Sarah. 'I'm Felicity Morton.'

'Welcome to Ingham Lacey,' said Sarah with what warmth she could muster.

'Gosh, it's a daunting old place,' said the girl with a shiver. 'And chilly, even on a warm day like this.'

'Haunted too,' said Alex, grinning evilly.

Big blue eyes goggled at him. 'Really?'

'Oh, yes. Some Cavalier chap died of his wounds in the priest-hole while the Roundheads were searching the place for him.' Alex turned to Sarah. 'Sir Edward Frome is supposed to walk at night in bloodstained shirt and breeches, isn't that right?'

'Absolute rot!' said the Colonel firmly as the girl stared in horror. He took her hand. 'You're frightening the little lady to death.'

'Little lady', thought Sarah, her five feet seven suddenly transformed to giantess proportions. 'It's just a story, Miss Morton. I've slept here alone countless times, and I've never seen young Ned's ghost—or anyone else's. Disappointing, really. Now if you'll excuse me I have work to do. If there's anything you lack,' she added to Alex, 'don't hesitate to contact me.'

'I hope not to trouble you—I've brought everything I need,' he said very deliberately, and Sarah inclined her head, said polite goodbyes and removed herself as quickly as she could without actually taking to her heels and running away.

Sarah shut herself away in the butler's pantry, ostensibly to resume some restoration work, but mainly to pull herself together in private. She'd pictured meeting Alex again far too often for comfort, but never in her wildest imaginings had it occurred to her that he might bring someone to live here with him. And if it had she wouldn't have pictured someone like Felicity Morton, who looked barely out of her teens. But that, of course, could well be the attraction. Dewy youth was irresistible to most men, and Alex, it seemed, was no exception. Maybe he looked on Felicity as clay to be moulded.

The thought affected her concentration badly. Normally Sarah left this kind of work for the winter season. But this winter she would be somewhere else, and the painting was only one of several jobs she was determined to complete before she left Ingham Lacey for good. To aid concentration she put a tape of opera duets in her portable stereo to blot out the thought of Alex and the cute Felicity as a pair—an arrangement, Sarah thought with fury, he'd managed to make at quite remarkable speed. It was only just over a fortnight since his departure from Ingham Lacey.

She sat suddenly still, staring blindly at the still life she was restoring. Her own acquaintance with him had been of even less duration. Having ended up in Alex Mackenzie's bed herself, she was in no position to censure young Felicity Morton for doing the same.

Sarah had been working determinedly for some minutes, when a shadow fell across the painting.

'Yes?' she said absently, her eyes on the portion of nectarine she was cleaning.

'Jack told me I'd find you here,' said a curt, familiar voice.

Sarah forced herself to put down her brush without haste, switched off the tape, and turned on her stool to face Alex. 'Is there something you need after all?' she said politely.

'Yes. Enlightenment.' He had changed his clothes, and looked formidable in khakis and an olive-green sweatshirt. 'Why the hell have you resigned? My father's convinced I've got something to do with it. And he's right, of course. You're running away because I'm moving in.'

'I shan't leave until the end of summer. I'd hardly call it running away,' she pointed out coolly.

'Whatever you call it, you're leaving because I'm coming here to live. Isn't that the truth?'

'Yes.' Sarah slid from the stool and stood erect, her eyes clashing with his.

'And when did you decide on this course of action?' he demanded. 'Let me guess. Was it by any chance in the early hours of the morning after the party?'

'No.'

Alex stared, taken aback. '*No?* When, then? Once you had time to think after I left?'

Sarah shook her head. 'I can't pinpoint my decision to an actual minute, but I came to it on the Friday evening before the party.'

He stared at her blankly. '*Before* the party?'

'That's right.'

To Sarah's immense satisfaction Alex looked nonplussed.

'Then why in hell's name did you let me make love to you that night?' he demanded in outrage.

She shrugged. 'Why not?'

'Don't be clever, Sarah.' His eyes glittered menacingly. 'Tell me the truth. I didn't take you by force, or coerce you in any way. You wanted what happened as much as I did—unless you're the most consummate actress in the entire world.'

'Which I'm not,' she assured him, feeling better by the minute. Alex had floored her completely by producing the nubile Felicity. Now the tables were turned.

'So tell me why!' he said urgently, taking a step towards her. For a moment Sarah thought he was going to seize her and shake the truth out of her, but the icy flash in her eyes stopped him in his tracks. '*Tell* me,' he commanded.

Sarah shrugged with feigned indifference. 'I was curious.'

'Curious!' He fought visibly for calm. 'If that's the case I can safely say I satisfied more than just your curiosity.'

'True,' she agreed, taking the wind out of his sails. 'It was a very informative experience all round.' She looked up at the sound of voices.

'Colonel Newby's giving Fliss the guided tour,' said Alex, and a moment later the girl came in, shivering in the skimpy vest-top.

'Brr!' she complained. 'It's jolly cold here, Alex. What on earth is it like in winter?'

The Colonel laughed. 'Bracing in the extreme, but don't worry, the private rooms are cosy enough.'

Felicity looked doubtful, then her eyes brightened as she caught sight of the half-cleaned painting on the worktop. 'Gosh, are you doing this, Miss Law? Look, Alex.'

'Miss Law is a lady of many talents,' agreed Alex smoothly, and took the girl's arm. 'Come on, Fliss; I feel the need for a drink. Won't you join us, Colonel? Miss Law?'

When both declined Alex shooed the girl ahead of him in a very unloverlike fashion, and the Colonel yawned.

'Right, then, Sarah, I'm off. See you in the morning. I'll leave you to lock up.'

Sarah tidied everything away, washed her hands, then went on her usual rounds, meeting Jack Wells on the ground floor.

'This is all done, Sarah,' he said, eyeing her. 'Liz was wondering if you'd like to come to supper tonight.'

'Could I come another night instead, Jack?' said Sarah. 'Thank Liz for me, but I'm a bit behind with the paperwork, and, to put her mind at rest, for once I've actually made a sort of casserole thing, which is simmering in my oven as we speak.'

'Then come on Friday instead.'

'Right I will,' she promised, and walked with Jack to the great oak door, which she locked with due ceremony. 'There. All done.'

Jack strolled with her across the lawn. 'By the way, did you know Alex was bringing someone with him, Sarah?'

'Not I!' She managed a cheerful grin. 'Bit of a turn-up for the books. Pretty girl.'

'A bit, well, young for him, isn't she?'

'Tut-tut, Jack,' said Sarah reprovingly. 'None of our business.'

'Liz hoped it was yours, you know.'

'Well, it ain't! See you tomorrow, Jack. And thank Liz.'

Sarah had a bath, towelled her hair, and sat down with a book to eat the casserole she'd put together that morning from a few slivers of chicken and a mound of fresh vegetables and herbs donated by Jack. She'd fully expected to find her appetite scotched by the appearance of young Felicity Morton, but the meal gained much piquancy from the memory of Alex's face at the discovery that she'd let him make love to her out of mere curiosity.

Sarah smiled coldly, then banished Alex—and Felicity—from her mind by concentrating on the administration for the concert due to take place the following month. She was in the kitchen, making coffee afterwards, when the noise she dreaded most frightened her to death, her blood running cold as the smoke alarms in the cottage went off with a concerted shrieking which galvanised her into instant action.

The routine was automatic from countless drills. Knowing Jack would make straight for the house, Sarah made a swift examination of the cottage, not expecting to find the cause but needing to make sure. To her relief the occupants of both the holiday cottages were out for the evening. As she used her master key on the larger one Tim Sewell came running along the path.

'All clear in our place, Sarah.'

'Right.' She unlocked the second cottage. 'You check this one, I'll search the other. The fire brigade should be here soon.'

When nothing amiss was found at the stable block, Sarah and Tim raced over to the house.

Liz met them with her usual lack of fuss. 'Jack's already inside.'

Tim ran to join Jack, while Sarah raced to the butler's pantry with Liz. They collected wire trays and bubble wrap and tore up the main staircase to the drawing-room, where Sarah gathered up the priceless ceramic vases, working at desperate speed to wrap the pieces and lay them in trays that Liz could carry down to put on the grass near the stable block before racing back into the house for more.

Sarah had wrapped everything and had begun carrying trays down herself when she found Felicity on the lawn. 'Where's the fire?' she asked in excitement. 'It's not in the flat; I looked everywhere. Is it in the house?'

'We don't know yet,' said Sarah tersely. 'Where's Alex?'

'Gone to Sevenoaks to buy drinks.'

'Do you fancy giving a hand?'

'You bet!'

Janet Sewell hurried across the lawn to join them. 'My mother's just arrived to keep the boys indoors, much to their rage, so tell me what you want done, Sarah. Have they found any fire?'

'I don't think so; we'll just carry on until Jack says otherwise. We'll strip the drawing-room first.' Sarah sprinted back up the stairs, shouting instructions as to priorities. The four of them worked like beavers, making several trips with lighter pieces of furniture before the welcome sirens of the fire engines brought Sarah some relief. She kept expecting black smoke to billow from some part of the ancient building, and worked with her heart in her throat, unable to bear the thought of her beloved old house gutted by fire.

Within minutes experienced fire-fighters were searching the house from roof to crypt with Jack and Tim, while their colleagues waited outside, hoses connected in readiness. The women were advised to take a rest, and Sarah sagged down on the grass with the others, gasping for breath.

'I keep saying I'll go to aerobics classes,' panted Liz bitterly. 'Now I really will.'

'Take me with you,' groaned Janet, chest heaving. 'Are you all right, dear?' she asked Felicity.

'Fine!'

'How about you, Sarah?' asked Liz.

'I just wish they'd find out what started off the alarms,' said Sarah, and tensed as Alex came tearing across the lawn towards them.

'What the devil's going on?' he demanded.

'All the smoke alarms went off,' said Sarah, 'but so far they haven't found the source of the fire. They won't let us bring out any more stuff.'

'I've been helping,' said Felicity proudly. 'Gosh, I'm thirsty. I could eat a horse, too.' She gave Alex a cajoling smile. 'By the way, I hope there's more steak in the freezer. I couldn't get the hang of the grill in there. I'm afraid I burnt the two we brought with us.' Her eyes opened wide as the others stared at her. Her look was self-deprecating. 'I'm not much of a cook, but I wanted to surprise Alex...' She trailed off into silence as Alex choked back a curse and raced across the drawbridge, leaving the girl staring after him, bewildered.

'What did I say?' she asked.

'Felicity,' said Sarah gently, 'when you burnt the steaks there must have been a lot of smoke.'

Felicity pulled a face. 'A bit. I went to the loo and forgot the things were under the grill, but there were no flames or anything. The smell was awful so I opened the windows...' She halted, looking from one face to another, horror dawning in the wide blue eyes. 'Oh, no! You don't mean...?'

Sarah nodded, and explained that if one smoke alarm went off they all did.

A visible shudder of apprehension ran through Felicity as Alex reappeared from the gatehouse with the laughing group of fire-fighters. After they'd stowed their equipment away Alex shook the chief's hand, then strode across the drawbridge towards the little group on the lawn, his face grim.

'Oh, gosh,' quavered Felicity, grubby hands twisting together. 'He's furious.'

'It was an accident,' Sarah reassured her, and got wearily to her feet as Alex joined them. 'Everything sorted out?' she asked him.

'Yes. My apologies to you all.'

Felicity gulped, then said bravely, 'I'm the one who should apologise. I didn't realise I'd set all the alarms off. It never occurred to me—'

'It's my fault. I obviously didn't explain clearly,' said Alex, tight-lipped, plainly restraining himself with effort from saying more.

'Felicity worked like a Trojan to help us get this lot out here,' said Sarah quickly. There was a chorus of assent from Liz and Janet, both of them, Sarah noted with amusement, eager to deflect Alex's wrath from the girl.

They were a sweat-soaked, dishevelled bunch by this time, after their exertions in the warm, humid evening. Sarah's once white T-shirt was sticking to her, and her hair was hanging in rat's tails from its knot, something which obviously afforded Alex grim satisfaction as his eyes ran over her.

'I'm very grateful to you all. If it had been the real thing a remarkable quantity of valuables would have been saved.' He forced a smile. 'My turn to provide the muscles this time. I'll help put everything back. The ladies can retire with honour.'

'I'll help too,' said Felicity, eager to make reparation.

'No way!' Alex shook his head, eyeing her with hostility. 'You've done enough. Go on, run back to the flat and take a shower. I won't be long.'

Any antipathy Sarah might have felt towards the girl vanished as the small, disconsolate figure trudged across the drawbridge. 'Don't be too hard on her, Alex; she's very young. She had no idea what she'd started.'

'It's as well she's aware of what her carelessness *could* have started. Responsibility for one's actions is best learned early. It saves trouble later on,' he added deliberately, his eyes cold as they held hers. 'Right, ladies, I'm sure that between us Jack, Tim and I can get this lot back. Thank you once again. Please go off and have a well-earned rest.'

Janet and Liz were only too glad to agree, but Sarah shook her head. 'The ceramics are my own personal responsibility. I'll put those back myself.'

Alex was very obviously on the point of forbidding her to do any such thing, but Jack and Tim arrived, defusing the moment, and Janet and Liz hastily said their goodnights.

'Jack,' said Alex brusquely, 'come and lend weight to my argument. I think Sarah should leave the rest to us.'

To his evident surprise Jack and Tim shook their heads simultaneously. 'We can carry the trays of ceramics up to the rooms where they belong,' said Jack, 'but otherwise I'm not laying a finger on the things. Sarah'd have my hide if I broke anything, and Tim's only helping us out of the goodness of his heart. He's responsible for the garden only, not the house.'

'Talking of which I'd as soon get all this stuff off my lawn,' said Tim anxiously, eyeing the various articles lying on his beloved grass. He looked up at the sky. 'And pretty sharpish, too. Rain's forecast for later.'

His words kick-started them into action again, Sarah insisting on doing her share. It was very late by the time everything was back in place in the house, other than the ceramics, trays of which stood ready in various rooms for her to unpack.

'Leave the rest for the morning, Sarah,' Alex ordered. 'You look shattered.'

She shook her head. 'The house is open tomorrow. I'd rather do it tonight.'

'It's all right,' said Jack. 'I'll stay with her.'

'You'd better get back to the flat, Alex,' advised Sarah. 'Felicity was crying when you sent her off.'

'As well she might,' said Alex grimly, eyeing Sarah's colourless face. 'I suppose I'd better see that she hasn't got up to more mischief.'

'Please tell her that none of us blames her,' said Sarah with emphasis. 'She worked as hard as any of us, remember.'

Jack and Tim suddenly found something urgent to see to in another part of the house, leaving Sarah and Alex alone in the shadowy drawing-room.

'I wish you'd pack it in,' said Alex with sudden violence. 'You've got dark marks under your eyes, and you're as white as a sheet.'

'I always look pale when I'm hot,' she said matter-of-factly. 'Goes with the colouring.' Her eyes met his squarely. 'Please go back to Felicity and let me get on.'

'Was her arrival a surprise to you this afternoon?' he asked abruptly.

'Yes, it was,' she said with candour. 'But I'd already seen that the flat was tidy and clean linen supplied. Otherwise I'm not involved.'

'Don't I know it,' he said bitterly. 'You made that only too clear last time we spoke. Goodnight, then, Sarah. And for God's sake finish up here as soon as you can and get to bed.'

He turned away and strode from the room. Sarah heard him talking with Jack and Tim, and with a sigh began to remove the wrappings from a vase, feeling every bit as exhausted as she obviously looked.

It was gone midnight before everything was in place and the house locked up securely for the night. Jack had stayed with Sarah to the end, removing trays and wrappings as she worked. Afterwards he hurried back with her to the cottage through the rain Tim had forecast, and saw her safely through her kitchen door before he went off to the Lodge.

Sarah yanked her bedroom curtains shut to blank out her view of the house, then stood under a hot shower for a long time, sluicing away the sweat and dust of her exertions. Normally she slept with her bedroom curtains drawn back so that she could see the stars, but tonight when the windows went dark Alex would be in bed with Felicity.

A quick shiver ran through her at the thought. Felicity would naturally be eager to placate Alex for the embarrassment of the false alarm. And, as Alex had said, he was a normal man with a normal man's instincts. The girl was young and very, very pretty and was no doubt at this very moment soothing his anger away by pleasing him in bed. Why else would he have brought her here?

When Sarah got up next morning every muscle protested after her exertions of the night before. It was an effort to get over to the house in time, and all the stewards were agog to hear details of the disturbance. Sarah knew that most of the ladies were eager to know details about Felicity too, but none of them dared ask, particularly as Sarah was in a stern, withdrawn mood, due as much to weariness as to her disinclination to discuss anything to do with Alex Mackenzie. She confirmed that his guest's attempt at cooking had led to a call-out for the fire brigade, then changed the subject firmly.

There was no sighting of Alex or Felicity during the morning, much to Sarah's relief and the staff's disappointment. Sarah was kept busy with Colonel Newby, checking the entire house with the inventory, to make sure that in the hurry of getting everything back nothing had been damaged or put in the wrong place.

'Everything's in order, Sarah,' he said at lunchtime. 'Which means that you can take yourself off for the rest of the day, and tomorrow as well. I shan't expect you back until Friday morning before the house opens. I know you've had no time off while I was away, so no arguments, please.'

Far from arguing, Sarah smiled at him with radiant gratitude. A couple of days away from Ingham Lacey was a deeply attractive prospect, for more reasons than she cared to explain to the Colonel.

'I won't deny I could do with it,' she said with feeling.

'After last night's alarums and excursions I can well believe it.' He shook his head. 'Jack rang me after it was all over, but I should have been here, giving you a hand.'

'I apologise. I was so bent on getting things out I just didn't think. Worse than that, I didn't check the private quarters as Jack thought I had. I usually do, of course, but I assumed Mr Mackenzie would do his own check.'

He scanned her face shrewdly. 'Something wrong, Sarah?'

She shook her head. 'Nothing a good night's sleep won't put right.'

Sarah had a word with Jack, gave him her sister's telephone number, went back to the cottage, packed a few things and got in the car to head for London and her sister's flat. The long drive to Gloucestershire through pouring rain had no appeal, much as she'd have liked some pampering from her parents. And for the time being she badly needed time on her own. Fortunately Jane had flown to Italy with the latest man in her life only the previous Saturday, having told Sarah she was free to use the flat whenever she wanted. Jane had given her a key months before when she'd moved in, so now all that was necessary was to buy some food in Sevenoaks *en route* to London, hole up in the flat and get some sleep undisturbed by dreams of Alex Mackenzie.

When Sarah reported to Colonel Newby's office in the gatehouse he rose with a smile to greet her, telling her she looked more like the Sarah he knew.

'I thought you were sickening for something when you left, you know.' He waved her to a chair. 'I'll ring the restaurant and get some coffee sent over while we go over the plans for the concert.'

There was no mention of Alex or Felicity, and since Sarah couldn't bring herself to ask it was left to Jack to tell her later that no one was in residence in the flat for the time being.

'Alex is coming back tomorrow, but little Miss Morton isn't, apparently,' he said, avoiding Sarah's eyes. 'I slept there last night.'

'Really?' she said casually. 'That was a short stay.'

'Liz is expecting you for supper tonight, remember,' he warned. 'No excuses.'

Sarah grinned. 'None intended. I'll be glad to come. Cooking isn't one of my talents.'

'You've got too many others to worry about that,' said Jack, to her surprise. 'I'll tell Liz about eightish, shall I?'

The cleaning team had weekends off, but Sarah spent a few hours on her own in the house on the Saturday morning to clean the upholstery on as much furniture as she could manage. The outer conservation work on the north-east walls created dust no matter how carefully the builders worked, and removing it from ancient, delicate furnishing fabrics was something Sarah preferred to do herself with a small hand vacuum cleaner. She worked with a net cover fitted over the head to avoid drawing out loose threads of fabric, hovering the machine over each piece in turn.

It was a tedious, time-consuming task, and Sarah felt pleased with a job well done as she made a leisurely tour of the house afterwards, noting that Liz had put in some time when she'd been away. Her attentions were apparent on the gleaming wood surfaces in every room.

Sarah sighed. Everyone worked as a team here. She would miss them. But the die had been cast now. She'd sent applications to the National Trust and English Heritage, even to Cadw, its Welsh counterpart, and with luck there might be a job for her somewhere now that she had three years of invaluable experience behind her to add to her qualifications. Though there would be no strings pulled for her this time. And before she left Ingham Lacey there were things to be done.

She went back to the cottage, made herself a sandwich and a cup of coffee, read the paper for a while, then recrossed the lawn to the butler's pantry, put a tape in her cassette player and settled herself on her stool under the north light of the window to resume work on the still life she was restoring.

As she had done all morning, no matter how hard she tried to divert her mind into different channels, Sarah couldn't help wondering why Felicity's stay had been so short. Surely Alex hadn't tired of the girl so rapidly? Or had his embarrassment and anger outweighed the poor girl's physical attributes? Whatever the reason the end result only confirmed Sarah's wisdom in removing herself from Alex Mackenzie's vicinity. She had no desire to join the legion of women who caught his fancy for a while before he got bored and went on to the next.

'I thought I'd find you here,' said Jack, behind her.

Sarah turned with a smile.

'Can't you just do nothing now and again, Sarah?' he demanded, leaning on the counter to peer at the oil. 'Looks good, though.'

'It's coming up well,' she agreed with satisfaction. 'Great meal last night, Jack. How you manage to keep your weight down on Liz's cooking I can never understand.'

'Actually I came to ask you a favour, Sarah.'

'Ask away,' she said, applying a brush delicately to a cluster of grapes.

'Could you possibly spend the night here, Sarah?' He cleared his throat noisily, looking rather embarrassed. 'Alex rang to say he won't be here until tomorrow night; he's got something on in London. And, well, I've booked a table at the Pheasant for Liz and me. It's our wedding anniversary. I thought Alex would be here, you see, and I don't like to bother the Colonel.'

'Say no more,' said Sarah, patting his hand. 'Of course I'll sleep over here.' But in the spare bedroom, she added silently. 'You go off and have a great evening.'

Later, Sarah made herself some sandwiches and took them with her to the flat to eat in front of a film on the television. It was a tense thriller, and she exclaimed with annoyance when the phone rang just as the police were closing in on the killer. She switched off the television and picked up the phone, her hand shaking when she heard Alex's voice in response to her hello.

'Sarah?' he said in surprise. 'Alex. I thought Jack was in the flat tonight?'

'It's his wedding anniversary,' she said with creditable calm. 'I volunteered to stay here instead.'

'Why the devil didn't he say so?' There was a pause. 'I'm trying to track down a folder I've mislaid. I'm hoping against hope I've left it in the bedroom there. Would you mind having a look?'

'Of course not.'

'It's an ordinary buff folder, pretty scruffy, with just a few notes and things, but some of the information is confidential.'

'Hold on.' Sarah put the phone down and went along the hall to the master bedroom. The folder, scruffy as Alex had said, but with the consortium logo in the corner to remove any possible doubt, had slid to the floor near the bed.

Sarah went back to the sitting-room and picked up the phone. 'It's here. Shall I send it on to you?'

'No need,' he said with relief. 'As long as I know it's safe it doesn't matter. If you'd put it in the drawer in the bedside table I'll collect it when I get back.'

'Right. Goodnight.'

'Sarah!' he said quickly. 'Don't hang up. How are you? Did you enjoy your break?'

'I'm fine and I did, yes. Very much.'

'Where did you go?'

'Only up to London. My sister's away on holiday; I stayed in her flat.'

'And did you contact one of those accommodating gentlemen ready to drop everything at your call?'

'Yes. As a matter of fact I did. We went clubbing. Made a pleasant change.'

'I was in London at the same time. I went back just after you left.'

'So I gather.'

'If I'd known where to contact you I'd have got in touch.'

'The aim,' said Sarah with deliberation, 'was to get away from this place and its associations for a day or two.'

'I thought you hardly ever forced yourself to leave it.'

'That was before you came.'

'Is my presence so intolerable to you, then?'

'No.'

'But you'd prefer my absence.'

'It's really not a problem. I'll be leaving soon myself.'

'You don't have to remind me.' He paused. 'Why the devil are you *doing* this, Sarah? Where did I go wrong? If it's Felicity you're thinking of I can explain that—'

'You really don't have to explain anything to me,' she said rapidly. 'It's absolutely none of my affair.'

'Right,' he snapped. 'Sorry to have troubled you. Goodnight.'

For a while her exchange with Alex ruined Sarah's evening. But at last she pulled herself together savagely, and, having missed the finale to the film, finished Jane's paperback thriller instead. To her intense satisfaction she woke up next morning to find that she'd achieved a few hours' sleep as well. She tidied up, feeling proud of herself, then took her belongings back to the cottage.

After breakfast she showered and put on the dress she'd worn to lunch with Alex. After a week of dull skies and occasional drizzle the day was hot and sunny and promised to be a scorcher, and she was in no mood for one of the sober outfits she normally wore when on duty. If Alex came back during open hours she needed to look good, totally unaffected by their conversation—or by Alex's flaunting of Felicity under her very nose.

It was a long way from the truth. Sarah still felt a pain whenever she thought of him with Felicity, but the breathing space in London had given her time to recover. To acquire a shell. And she wanted it to be the best-looking shell she could manage.

When the house was opened to the public at noon Sarah was on duty in the gatehouse, her eyes and lips brilliant, hair tied at the nape of her neck with a silk scarf, the dress satisfactorily cool as she welcomed visitors and directed them into the building. She made a point of visiting every room in the house at some point during the afternoon, pausing to answer questions *en route* here and there, giving additional information on the history of Ingham Lacey whenever it was required.

At just four in the afternoon, when the stream of visitors had begun to slow, as it always did by that time of day, Mrs Hayes, the senior steward, came looking for Sarah and found her in the Tudor chapel, engaged in a lively discussion on the brief reign of Edward the Sixth with an elderly gentleman in a crumpled linen suit.

'Miss Law,' said the steward apologetically, 'forgive me for interrupting, but a gentleman's asking for you downstairs.'

Sarah excused herself from the elderly visitor with a dazzling smile and went with Mrs Hayes down the stairs to the courtyard. 'Did he give his name?' she asked.

'I am sorry, I forgot to ask. He just said he was a friend, Sarah—he's waiting for you on one of the garden seats near the stable block.'

'Right.' Sarah walked across the courtyard and out past the gatehouse onto the drawbridge, shading her eyes against the sun. As she looked, a man got up from the seat furthest away and walked quickly towards her, his hair glinting bright in the sun.

'Martin!' said Sarah in surprise as he kissed her on both cheeks.

'I've escaped the bosom of my family for the entire afternoon,' he announced, smiling down at her.

Martin Dryden was still a very handsome man who looked ten years younger than the fifty Sarah knew him to be. His fair hair, worn slightly long and floppy, was as plentiful as ever, only lightly streaked with silver here and there, and the chiselled features were clear-cut, with no blurring of middle age yet to spoil them. He wore a white shirt open at the neck under a pale grey suit, and if there was a hint of weariness about the brilliant blue eyes it was only to be expected from the father of three small children.

'This is an unexpected pleasure,' said Sarah.

He nodded. 'No Isobel, no Jamie, no twins. Don't misunderstand,' he added, with the wry charm that Sarah had once found so irresistible, 'I love them all, but a day off from family life now and then is essential. If I'd achieved fatherhood earlier in life it might have been easier.'

'It's a miracle you didn't,' said Sarah bluntly, 'with all those girls hankering for your body through the years.'

'Ouch!' Martin winced theatrically, but he was flattered rather than offended, she knew well. 'But you, Sarah, were the first to appeal to me on a permanent basis—'

'Until Isobel came along.'

'Until Isobel,' he agreed gravely, and sighed. 'It was never my *intention* to hurt you, Sarah.'

'I know.'

But he had, just the same.

They fell into step, skirted the bowling green and made for the Italian garden. Martin, as usual, was drawn to the ancient pieces of statuary among the hedges, some of them Greek and Roman, brought from their places of origin when a son of the house made the Grand Tour in the time of George the Third. Groups of people strolled in the warm afternoon sunshine, or sat on rustic benches to enjoy the view of gardens and house set against a panorama of fields gold with rape and green with hops, with the conical shapes of oast houses punctuating the landscape.

'This is the most incredibly beautiful place,' said Martin, and made for an empty bench. 'I can understand your reluctance to tear yourself away from it. Let us sit and gaze at Ingham Lacey, and you shall tell me how life is treating you and I shall bore you with tales of numbers of teeth, and the extraordinary brilliance of my offspring. I shall even force you to look at photographs.'

'Oh, come on, Martin, you revel in fatherhood,' said Sarah, laughing.

'I do. But mainly because my clever wife earns enough to pay a full-time nanny. Marvellous creature by the name of Dinah. What we would do without her I can't imagine.' He turned the famous blue eyes on her for a long, analytical moment. 'What's the matter, Sarah?'

She stiffened. 'Why should anything be the matter?'

'I may have behaved appallingly towards you, but I know you well, and I have never stopped caring for you in my own peculiar way. Something is wrong. Is it a man?'

Sarah smiled carelessly. 'What else? But I'm coping.'

'Of course you are. The acme of efficiency and also very beautiful and Pre-Raphaelite in that dress—What have I said?' he added swiftly as she winced. 'I thought you liked Millais. Though today, in that delightful dress, you are more the spirit of Evelyn de Morgan's *Flora*—'

'I thought you'd given up lecturing, Martin! Anyway, I've changed.'

'I can see that.' He eyed her thoughtfully. 'But physically only for the better, if that's any consolation. You're a handsome creature, Sarah, particularly with the sun setting your hair on fire. But inside I fear the flame's burning a little low. Can I do anything to help? Give advice, provide a shoulder—or merely buy you tea and cakes?'

Sarah glanced at her watch. 'Give me five minutes to consult with the security officer, Jack Wells, then I shall give you tea in my cottage. Jack's wife is a fabulous cook. She not only gave me dinner the other evening, but sent me home with a box of her famed walnut biscuits.'

'Then I accept with alacrity,' said Martin, getting up to walk with her. 'Chez Dryden such delicacies tend to hie from Fortnum and Mason.'

'Did Isobel approve of your coming to see me?'

'To be truthful, Sarah, it was actually her idea. Isobel cares for you too, you know. At first her guilt about you almost outweighed her passion for me. And now look at us!' He chuckled. 'How civilised we are. Almost a *ménage à trois*. Or do I mean six, now Jamie and the twins are with us?'

'You're incorrigible!' said Sarah, laughing. 'Tell Isobel I think the latest book's tremendous. Wretched thing kept me awake all night because I couldn't put it down until I finished it.'

Sarah told Jack where she was going, then took Martin back to the cottage. 'We'll have tea in the kitchen, if you don't mind, and leave the door open to what breeze there is. The last of the visitors will have gone by this time, so there's no danger of anyone wandering in, thinking my house is part of the tour.'

They sat at the kitchen table companionably, drinking endless cups of tea and finishing off all Liz's cookies while Martin displayed the promised photographs and related the latest anecdotes about his children, no longer troubling to hide his paternal pride.

'I almost forgot,' he said at last. 'I'm to bid you to a soirée at the house of Dryden. Isobel's agent has sold her latest book to a television company. That girl who wins all the awards is cast as the Victorian lady missionary in darkest Africa. So erotic, you know, all those corsets and starched white underwear.' Martin smiled. 'We are celebrating.'

'As well you might. Give Isobel my congratulations. And, thank you, I'd love to come,' said Sarah with enthusiasm.

'Good. Isobel will send you a card.' He sighed. 'Heigh-ho, time to return to the nest. Hard though it may be for you to imagine, I rather enjoy bathtime with my little terrors. May I retire upstairs for a moment or two first?'

Sarah directed him to the bathroom, then sat down again at the kitchen table to drink another cup of tea.

'Sarah!' said a voice behind her.

Sarah turned, resigned, to see Alex in the open doorway. She got up, pinning a serene smile of enquiry to her face. 'Come in. Is there something I can do for you?'

'You know damn well there is,' he said with barely controlled violence, starting towards her as though he meant to seize her in his arms. Then he stopped dead as Martin sauntered into the kitchen, brandishing the miniature painting in his hand.

'I found this charming little trifle on your dressing table—' he began, then halted, a quizzical smile on his handsome face.

'Martin,' said Sarah quickly, 'I don't believe you've met Alex Mackenzie. Alex, this is Professor Dryden.'

Both men said the usual things, Alex's face wooden as he took the hand Martin offered.

'I'm sorry I intruded,' he said distantly. 'It wasn't important. I'll see you another time, Sarah.' He nodded to Martin, showed his teeth in a smile, then strode from the kitchen into the garden.

'My timing is obviously disastrous,' said Martin, and put the painting on the table. 'Who, exactly, is Alex Mackenzie, other than a man who very obviously lusts after you?'

'Nonsense.' Sarah clattered cups as she cleared away. 'He's the Mackenzie of Mackenzie Holdings, the consortium which owns Ingham Lacey.'

'I'm sure he's everything you say, Sarah, but he lusts after you just the same.' Martin subjected her to a piercing blue scrutiny. 'And my instincts—which are never wrong in such matters—tell me his feelings are very much requited.'

'Rubbish,' said Sarah, wielding a tea-towel energetically.

'My darling child, don't be repetitious. The air between you fairly crackled with electricity.'

Sarah hesitated, blinked rapidly, then to her horror dissolved into tears. Martin, vastly experienced in such matters, simply took her in his arms, murmuring comfort, stroked her hair and waited until the storm passed.

'I'm so sorry,' said Sarah thickly, detaching herself. She took some kitchen paper from a roll and blew her nose prosaically while Martin watched in wry amusement.

'Do you know, Sarah, that I have never witnessed your tears before, not even—?'

'Not even when you dumped me for another woman,' she finished for him, and he winced theatrically.

'Blunt, but true.' Martin smoothed her hair back from her damp forehead. 'Does this mean that you are in love with the formidable gentleman thirsting to black my eye just now?'

'Yes,' she said thickly.

'Where's the problem, then, my sweet? He obviously feels the same way about you—'

'No, he doesn't.' Sarah shrugged, in command of herself once more. 'He wants us to be lovers, yes, but it's better I hurt now a bit than a lot later when he's had enough.' She looked him in the eye. 'I speak from experience, Martin.'

'Alas, I know you do, Sarah.' He frowned. 'But it could be different this time.'

She shook her head. 'Even his mother says he runs like a hare at the mention of anything permanent. And when I said no he proved my point pretty conclusively by installing a luscious—and very young—blonde in his flat here.'

'A gentleman of resource! Was his motive to make you jealous, by any chance?'

'If it was he succeeded,' said Sarah bitterly. She pointed at the miniature painting. 'He's an architect by training, but he's quite an artist, too. He did that.'

'Did he now? Very cleverly done. Brilliant brushwork. Where did he see you dreaming like that, I wonder?'

Sarah told him about the concert and her first encounter with Alex. 'But then I had no idea who he was.'

'Was it love at first sight?'

'Martin, stop it!' said Sarah impatiently. 'Anyone would think you wrote the romantic novels, not your wife.'

'My apologies. And, speaking of Isobel, it's high time I returned to her,' he said in a hurry, looking at his watch. He took Sarah in his arms and kissed her cheek. 'Come to the party. Bring a friend, if you like.'

She smiled, detaching herself. 'I might, at that. I'll ask Ben Ferris—you remember Ben?'

Martin frowned. 'You mean the disruptive young man who tried to woo you away from me in the old days?' He sighed. 'Oh, very well. Anything to please you, my darling Sarah. Give me his address and I'll get Isobel to send him an invitation.'

Sarah went back to the house once Martin had gone, and made her usual rounds in the dim, empty upper rooms, turning out lights as she went. She caught sight of herself, looking wraith-like in the series of dim, gilt-framed mirrors which a long-ago owner had brought back from Florence. In her pale, diaphanous dress, with her hair loose, she could well have been some ghostly apparition herself, she thought drily, then froze as a face appeared behind hers in the dark mirror.

'I thought I'd find you here,' said Alex.

Sarah turned to face him. 'You startled me.'

His smile was derisive. 'Did you think I was Ned Frome come to haunt you?'

'No. I don't believe in spectres from the past.' Those in the present were trouble enough, she thought wryly.

'I apologise for my intrusion earlier,' he said stiffly. 'Though I had a valid reason for seeking you out. I came to beg a few minutes of your time. I have something to propose.'

Sarah stood very still. 'Go on.'

'Not here,' said Alex quickly. 'When you've finished locking up will you come over to the flat? I'd like you to listen to what I've got to say.'

'Very well. I'll be about ten minutes. I think Jack's finished down below.'

When Alex had gone Sarah went on with her usual routine with increasing tension, wondering what he meant by a proposal. She locked the great oak door, then retraced her footsteps and mounted the worn, winding stone stair to the flat. Alex let her in quickly, as though he'd been listening for her knock.

'Will you have a drink, Sarah?' He waved at the laden silver tray on a drum table beneath the latticed windows. 'Wine?'

'I'd rather have fruit juice, if you have it.'

Alex waved her to a chair. 'I'll fetch some from the kitchen.'

Sarah's tension mounted to unbearable proportions as she waited for him to return, all kinds of wild conjectures chasing through her mind.

Alex came back with a jug of orange juice clinking with ice, and a glass tankard of beer. He filled a glass with juice and handed it to her.

'Thank you.' Sarah sipped gratefully. 'It's a thirsty sort of day.'

'Eventful, too,' he remarked, and sat down on the nearest chair, looking at her morosely. 'Or do old flames of yours turn up regularly?'

'I meet with the others in London,' she said, unruffled. 'But Martin often comes here. He's an art historian, remember, and his wife writes historical novels. They came together last time to gather some material for a book Isobel set in the sixteenth century. The records here are remarkably detailed.'

'But today he came alone,' said Alex without inflection.

'Yes.'

There was a pause.

'Why was he in your bedroom?' demanded Alex suddenly, as though the words choked him.

'Isn't that my business?' she returned with dangerous quiet.

Alex's eyes gleamed coldly. 'It could be mine, professionally speaking, of course. The consortium would hardly approve of dalliance in working hours on the part of one of its employees.'

'But since I'll soon no longer be an employee it's hardly relevant!'

'You might find it so if we withhold a reference,' he cut back.

Sarah's chin lifted. 'That's entirely up to you,' she said coldly.

Silence fell, lengthened, thickened and quivered in the air between them until suddenly, Alex got up and went to the tray to seize the jug of fruit juice. 'Will you have more of this?'

Sarah longed to say no, but the exchange between them had left her mouth dry. 'Thank you.' She held out her glass with a hand not quite as steady as she would have liked, her only consolation the fact that Alex's was no better as he poured the fruit juice.

He sat down, thrusting a hand through his hair impatiently. 'Sarah, I'm sorry. That was the male animal talking. Mackenzie the employer knows damn well you're good at your job. A reference—couched in glowing terms—is yours, verbally or written, any time you want it.'

Sarah relaxed slightly. 'Thank you.'

Alex locked his eyes with hers. 'But I hope you won't want it. Be honest, Sarah. I'm to blame for your decision to resign. Ingham Lacey isn't big enough for both of us. Isn't that the truth?'

Sarah nodded slowly, making no attempt to deny it. 'Yes. It is.'

'So if I went would you stay?'

This time the silence was even longer as Sarah came to terms with the form Alex's proposal was obviously going to take. She quelled the stabbing pain of her disappointment, survived it, then looked up from her drink to meet Alex's steel-bright eyes. 'If you leave and I stay you're back to square one with the problem of this flat.'

'Not if you consent to take it over.'

Sarah put down her drink carefully and leaned forward. 'You mean you want me to live here as a permanent arrangement?'

'It was my father's idea,' he said stiffly. 'Or possibly even my mother's. Dad was very put out by your letter of resignation. From his point of view you are the ideal person for the job. Efficiency is easy to engage, he told me. Finding someone with your particular wholehearted devotion to the place is a different matter.'

'How very nice of him.'

Alex's mouth twisted. 'So my mother—who is by no means the featherhead she's at pains to make out she is—solved the entire problem at one stroke. I vacate the flat, you move in, and your cottage is handed over to the assistant gardener we intend to hire to help Tim.'

'But where will you go?' asked Sarah, frowning.

'Back where I belong,' he said morosely. 'My place in Chelsea is still on the market. I'll withdraw it.' He raised an eyebrow. 'Well, Sarah Law? What do you say? Do you need time to think it over?'

For pride's sake Sarah said yes. 'You can have your answer in the morning,' she said crisply.

'I'll knock on your door early in the morning, then— I need to be off just after seven to chair a meeting in the City.'

Sarah got up, and Alex went to the door to open it for her.

'Goodnight,' she said politely.

'Goodnight.'

For a moment Sarah was sure he would take her in his arms. She could feel the tension and heat in his body across the foot of space that separated them, but Alex stood motionless, hands clenched at his sides, and she walked without haste through the door and into the hall outside. She turned to look at him.

'By the way, Martin had gone up to the bathroom for very obvious reasons this afternoon. He caught sight of the painting as he passed my bedroom door.' Sarah smiled faintly. 'He was deeply impressed by the workmanship.'

CHAPTER TEN

AS THE stable clock struck seven Alex's peremptory knock on her door brought Sarah tumbling out of bed in consternation. She threw on a dressing gown and ran barefoot downstairs, wielding a hairbrush as she went, before opening the back door on the daunting formality of Alex Mackenzie in dark suit, striped silk tie and dazzling white shirt.

'Sorry,' she said breathlessly, 'I woke early and dozed off again. Come in.'

'Good morning.' His face relaxed a little at her quickly smothered yawn.

'I'm not all here yet,' she said candidly.

'I hope I'm dealing with the part ready to give me an answer,' he said, unsmiling.

'Yes, you are,' she replied in kind. 'On the terms you described last night I'll be very happy to stay here as housekeeper. When do you want me to move into the flat?'

'Whenever you like. My stuff is all packed and stowed in the car. I had no intention of staying, whatever your decision. The flat's all yours.' Alex stared through the window at the house shrouded in its veil of morning mist. 'A romantic impulse on my part, but never a practical arrangement,' he said bleakly.

'You make me feel guilty, as though I'm turning you out.'

Alex turned back to her, his eyes boring into hers. 'If you feel any guilt, Sarah, it should be for letting me make love to you. The real eviction was afterwards when you slammed the gates of paradise in my face.' His mouth twisted. 'Hell, listen to me! It's time I got back to the real world for good. This place is affecting my speech patterns. Goodbye, Sarah. Who knows? Perhaps we'll run into each other at some future concert.'

'Perhaps we will,' she said quietly, above the thunder of her heartbeat. 'Goodbye.'

'Sarah.' Alex moved a fraction nearer. 'About Felicity—'

'Don't!' Sarah moved back a step in physical and mental retreat. 'Your—your private life is absolutely nothing to do with me.'

Alex's jaw clenched, then without another word he turned on his heel and went out. Sarah watched him from the window as he paused to have a word with Tim, wishing, not for the first time, that things could have been different. She shook her head irritably and turned away to fill the kettle, then went up to shower while it boiled. Today was the first day of the rest of her life, and if Alex would be missing from it she would adjust to the loss eventually. She'd done it before with Martin. She could do it again with Alex Mackenzie.

Once she was used to it Sarah liked the idea of living in the private quarters of the house. Her morale boosted sky-high by the wave of relief displayed by every member of the staff when they heard she was staying, she took advantage of offers of help, and was soon installed in the spare bedroom of the flat, with some of her own belongings distributed through the rooms to add a personal touch.

'Why aren't you using the main bedroom?' asked Liz as she helped make up the bed with Sarah's linen.

'My sheets won't fit the bed. Besides, it's cosier in here and I can see right across the garden to the cottages, in case I get homesick for mine.'

Liz looked unconvinced. 'The other bedroom has windows on two sides—you can see in two directions at once.'

Sarah laughed as she punched the last pillow into place. 'Nevertheless, Mrs Wells, I prefer this one.'

'I don't know how you can bear it here alone at night, whichever bedroom you sleep in.' Liz shuddered. 'I wouldn't for a fortune.'

'And now I'm here Jack won't have to either,' Sarah reminded her. 'If Alex Mackenzie had stayed on he'd have been away as much as he was here.'

'I wonder why he suddenly decided against it?' Liz frowned. 'In the beginning I thought you two were getting on like a house on fire—' she crossed her fingers '—if you'll pardon the expression! Then next thing we knew he'd brought young Felicity here. Not that she stayed long. Is that still on?'

'No idea,' said Sarah dismissively. 'Nothing to do with me.'

'If you say so.' Liz went over to the dressing table to look out across the empty garden. 'I love it here on closed days. It's so peaceful. I say, Sarah, this is exquisite! Who did it?'

Sarah turned to see Liz staring, entranced, at the angel portrait. 'A friend. Not a professional artist. It's his hobby.'

'He must be pretty keen if he thinks of you as an angel! Is this one of the faithful swains you see when you're in London?'

Sarah made a non-committal noise and began folding sweaters into drawers. 'Talking of angels, Liz, fancy making some coffee?'

A fortnight after Alex's departure a string quartet came to give a concert at Ingham Lacey. On the night, when visitors began to arrive, Sarah was buoyed up, as she had been for days, by the hope that Alex would be among them. She welcomed the concertgoers with her usual warmth and courtesy, secretly keyed up to concert pitch, like the waiting instruments, as she directed people to their places in the chairs arranged in the Great Hall that afternoon. As the minutes ticked by her hopes began to fade, then just before the concert was due to start Alex's parents came hurrying across the courtyard. But with no sign of their son.

'Sarah!' said Mrs Mackenzie warmly, patting her hand. 'How beautiful you look in that clever green dress.'

'Hello, my dear,' said her husband, close behind. He smiled benignly at Sarah. 'I'm glad you chose to stay as housekeeper. You made the right decision. Are you happy in the flat?'

'I love living there,' said Sarah with truth, and beckoned one of the stewards to hand over two programmes, glad that the music was about to begin. 'I'll see you in the interval—I think you'll enjoy the selection.'

Sarah hardly heard the music in the first half. She stared up at the worn, familiar tapestry, utterly shattered by her own disappointment. Until now she hadn't realised just exactly how much she'd hoped Alex would be here. Illogical, she told herself savagely. She had done the rejecting this time. And Alex had made it stringently clear that he wasn't the type to beg.

'My son sent you a message, Sarah,' said Alexander Mackenzie during the interval.

She smiled, glad that her skin never betrayed the heat she could feel rising from her toes to the roots of her hair. 'Really?'

Ellen Mackenzie nodded happily. 'He's found a woman who can repair the bed-hangings in the Chinese bedroom.'

'How—how good of him to remember,' said Sarah, secretly reeling from her second blow of the night. 'When can she start?'

'Not until you put the house to bed for the winter, I'm afraid,' said Ellen regretfully. 'She's working in some castle up north at the moment—I can't remember the name. But she'll be available by autumn.' Keen blue eyes looked into Sarah's. 'You look tired, dear. This place must be a lot of work.'

'But very rewarding. And with Colonel Newby back to manage the estate part it's a lot easier.' Sarah turned to Alexander Mackenzie. 'Have you seen the progress on the east wall?'

'I certainly have—that's why we cut it a bit fine to get in here before the concert started!' He nodded approvingly. 'The builders are doing a great job.'

'They've been working long hours lately,' said Sarah. 'The foreman's keen to utilise this dry spell.'

They chatted together for a minute or two more, then Jack signalled that the second half was due to start and Sarah began shepherding people back into the Great Hall.

After Alex's non-appearance at the concert Sarah's adjustment programme had returned to square one. Hang in there, she told herself as she lay sleepless in bed that night. Stop feeling sorry for yourself and look forward to the Drydens' party. Isobel's parties were usually evenings to remember. She had a talent for entertaining, always managing to invite the right mix to make the evening a success. She's also younger than me, thought Sarah, and she's produced two best-selling novels, three children, and Martin is as besotted with her now as he was the moment they first met.

Ah, but I could have had Alex Mackenzie for a lover, thought Sarah. Too late to moan about it now he had Felicity, of course. But after only two weeks without seeing or hearing from him it seemed idiotic to have turned him down. They were two adult people with no ties. It would have been easy enough to keep the arrangement separate from Ingham Lacey. They could have spent time together in London on her days off and no one would have been any the wiser. And she would have been a lot happier than she was now.

Sarah sighed, fast beginning to suspect that a relationship with Alex, however brief, might well have been worth the inevitable anguish when it was over. Their one night of sheer perfection just wasn't enough to last her for the rest of her life. Of course it was perfectly possible that she might meet someone else one day, she reminded herself. She pulled the bedcover up under her chin, despite the warmth of the night, suddenly cold with the knowledge that if she didn't take Alex on his terms she wanted no one else on any terms at all.

At the end of a particularly gruelling open day the following Friday, with a record number of visitors, Sarah retired to the flat with relief when she'd made sure all was secure, a routine which took longer than usual because Jack was away for the weekend. Too tired to start preparations for supper, she sat in a chair by one of the windows, watching Janet and Tim at their watering. Sarah leaned out of the window and Tim called up to remind her that they were off to Wiltshire to his parents' in a few minutes.

'Are you sure you'll be all right if I stop there overnight?' he said. 'Jan's staying there with the boys for a few days but I'll be back first thing.'

'Of course I'll be all right—have a lovely time, Janet,' called Sarah, then sat back in her chair to gaze at the new moon, which was a tiny sliver of light on the horizon, like a paring from a baby's fingernail . . . Suddenly Sarah jerked awake from a doze, sure she'd heard a noise.

She laughed away the icy little chill running down her spine. Surely she wasn't succumbing to nerves about poor Ned Frome? Besides, he was supposed to be a very quiet young spectre. According to legend he just appeared in the gallery in his bloodstained finery and vanished through the panelling. Sarah got up and went to investigate. She hurried through the darkened house, gallery included, switching lights on and off, forced herself to go down to the crypt, and by the end of her tour felt thoroughly on edge for once. But there were no intruders in the house, spectral or otherwise, just as she'd expected.

She locked her door behind her, felt better when she looked across at the lights in the holiday lets, switched on a few extra lights in the flat, then went to the kitchen to cook supper. When she heard the same noise again she realised rather sheepishly that it obviously came from outside. Sarah leaned through the open window and saw a figure in familiar overalls and hard hat in the distance near the entrance gates.

'Dave?' she called. 'Is that you?'

He raised a hand in acknowledgement and pointed to the car park to indicate that he was just off. Vastly relieved, Sarah returned to her supper.

After her doze in the twilight Sarah had no great expectation of falling asleep quickly, though these days, since Alex's departure, broken nights were part of life. She read for some time when she was in bed, and switched off her light at last with reluctance, glad that tomorrow the house was closed to the public and she could take some time off in the afternoon. She dozed off eventually but woke again with a start in total darkness, depressed when the luminous hands on her watch told her it was only a little after two. She groaned and punched her pillow, turned it over to find a cool spot, then shot upright, the hairs on her neck standing on end as she heard something.

Sarah sat very still, listening intently, then heard the noise again—no figment of her imagination, but the chink of metal on stone, and this time it was accompanied by the faint but unmistakable sound of human effort. She slid out of bed in the dark, not daring to put on a light. Then she breathed in sharply as it dawned on her just why it was so dark. The security lights weren't working.

Sarah flew across the room for her mobile phone and rang Colonel Newby.

'What is it, Sarah?' he asked swiftly.

'The security lights aren't working, and I can hear something outside, possibly coming from the Italian garden,' she said urgently. 'Sorry to bother you.'

'No bother. Jack's away, of course.'

'So's Tim, remember, just for tonight.'

He gave a muffled curse. 'Sod's law, Sarah. I'm on my way. Ring the police, please.'

Sarah contacted the police, then pulled on her dressing gown, found her espadrilles, and let herself out very quietly by the kitchen door, feeling her way in the dark. She picked her way down the stairs, then crossed the moat bridge at the back of the house to find the five-barred gate near the shop wrenched off its hinges. Someone, it was obvious, had driven a vehicle through into the grounds.

She blazed with sudden temper. Whoever it was wouldn't get out so easily. She heaved the gate back into place, propping it so that at first glance it looked shut, then whirled round with a gasp as she saw a dark shape coming towards her. As the shape edged nearer along the gravel drive she saw that it was a truck of some kind with its headlights off, and, giving herself no time to think, Sarah darted in front of it, her arms outstretched. There was a horrendous squeal of brakes as the truck swerved to avoid her, then a bang as it crashed into the gate. The truck swerved and teetered, and the door of the cab swung open, knocking Sarah to the ground, as the vehicle toppled over on its side and its contents crashed out on the gravel with enough noise to wake the dead just as two police cars came racing to the gate, with Colonel Newby's car close behind.

Sarah crawled to her hands and knees shakily, glad of Colonel Newby's strong arms as he helped her to her feet.

'Are you all right, my dear?' he demanded urgently. 'Let me take you in the house—'

'Not until I know what happened,' said Sarah urgently, shocked by the youth of the intruders as their faces were picked out by three sets of headlights. There were three of them, all protesting hysterically as they were led to a squad car. Miraculously, none of them appeared injured.

A police sergeant came to check on Sarah. 'I've called a doctor, miss. How do you feel?'

'I don't need a doctor,' she protested.

'Just routine, Miss Law. Best to check you over.'

'What happened?' she asked. 'The truck—'

'The truck's a wreck—it'll be towed away shortly,' the sergeant assured her. 'But thanks to you the stone artifacts are safe—as far as we can tell they weren't even damaged when the truck turned over.'

'Which did they take?' demanded Sarah. 'Not the Roman ones!'

'No, Sarah,' said the Colonel soothingly. 'They concentrated on the smaller pieces—urns, mostly. But they overloaded the truck, and it turned over when they swerved to avoid you. Lean on me; you must be feeling shaky.'

'I'm fine,' she assured him. 'Who were they?'

'A young local lad was the instigator,' said the sergeant. 'He told his pals how easy it would be to get in here and make off with stuff from the garden. The other two are still in school—cried like babies when we collared them. The ringleader's an apprentice electrician, works for the firm who installed the new security lights. He put them out of action earlier on, apparently.'

Sarah groaned. 'In overalls and a hard hat, no doubt, looking just like one of the workmen on the restoration. What an idiot I was! I actually *saw* him earlier. I thought he was the foreman. I even spoke to him. He just waved and sauntered off.'

'Cheeky little devil! He borrowed his father's pick-up, collected his mates, then they came back here when they thought no one would be about, took the gate off the hinges and pushed the vehicle along, as near as they could get it to the Italian garden.'

Sarah put a hand to her throbbing head. 'I feel such a fool—I can't believe I slept through it.'

'But you didn't, Sarah,' said the Colonel comfortingly. 'If you hadn't come on the scene when you did they might have pulled it off.' He chuckled. 'Now I know you're all right, I can see the funny side of it. You frightened them to death.'

'Really?' She cheered up slightly. 'How?'

'These are local boys, my dear, who believe Ingham Lacey is haunted. When a figure in white materialised in front of them in the darkness they crashed the truck in pure terror. Unfortunately they knocked you over in the process.'

Shortly afterwards Sarah was installed on a sofa in the sitting-room, drinking tea the Colonel had insisted on making after the sergeant returned to the car park with a constable to await the tow-truck and the doctor. Harriet Parker, a brisk, efficient young woman whom Sarah sometimes consulted, arrived a few minutes later, pronounced the patient free from concussion, dressed the cut on her temple, bound up a sprained wrist, and checked her all over for bruises. She gave Sarah some mild painkillers and told her to take it easy for a day or two.

'I don't like to leave you alone here in the circumstances, Sarah,' said Colonel Newby when they were finally alone. 'On the other hand it doesn't seem quite the thing for me to stay, either.'

Sarah chuckled. 'You go on home, Colonel. I'll be fine.'

Once she'd heard him lock the outer door behind him Sarah took herself off to bed, switched on her radio for company, then propped herself up on the pillows to watch the dawn. She dozed off at last, and woke in full sunshine to find herself looking up into a familiar, cheerful face.

'Mrs Hayes!'

'Good morning. How are you, my dear? The Colonel rang me, so I called at his house to collect the key to the flat. He's worried about you.'

'Oh, Mrs H, I'm so sorry. It's your day off!'

'I would have been very cross if he hadn't called me,' declared Mrs Hayes. 'I'll go and make you some breakfast. You look a bit the worse for wear, Sarah.'

'I've felt better,' admitted Sarah. 'Did he tell you what happened?'

'Only the barest outline.' The woman beamed. 'When I've brought your breakfast I want every last detail!'

Sarah submitted to being fussed over for most of the morning. Mrs Hayes tidied up the sitting-room, changed the sheets on the bed while Sarah was in the bath, then made a salad to leave in the fridge for the patient's lunch, and finally agreed to go home and leave Sarah to a nap.

When Colonel Newby arrived later, bearing a sheaf of roses, Sarah was up and dressed, and apart from a developing black eye looked none the worse for her adventure. She assured him her headache was subsiding, and that the following day she'd be ready to get back to work.

He said something noncommittal, and told her he'd call again in the morning. 'My wife sends her love, by the way, along with these roses from the garden. She's very anxious about you. She would have come with me, but it's not one of her good days.'

Sarah buried her face in the roses, then looked up with a smile. 'Thank her for me; they're beautiful. I'll come and see her on my next free day.'

'She'll like that.'

Tim was the next to come knocking on the door. 'Are you all right, Sarah?' he asked. 'I've just got back. The Colonel told me what happened—I *would* have to miss all the excitement. Wow, what a shiner!'

After an interlude with Tim, who assured her he was on hand any time if she needed anything, Sarah watched some cricket on television, until Dr Parker came to check up on her. The doctor commiserated with her over the ripening black eye, but otherwise agreed that Sarah was none the worse for her nocturnal experience. At some peremptory knocking on the outer door Dr Parker said goodbye, promising to let in Sarah's visitor on her way out.

Alex came into the room like a whirlwind. 'Sarah! Are you all right?' he demanded.

'Why, Alex—this is a surprise.' She scrambled to her feet involuntarily, then regretted it as her eye throbbed painfully at the sudden move. 'How—how kind of you to come.'

'I dropped everything to drive down here when I heard. The Colonel rang my father to tell him what happened.' He glared at her. 'What in the name of all that's wonderful possessed you to go out alone in the dark? You could have been killed, woman!'

Sarah, deeply resentful at being addressed as 'woman', glared back as well as she could with only one good eye. 'I had no intention of letting the thieves get away with anything. The house is partly my responsibility, remember—'

'It's not worth risking your life for, Sarah,' he said roughly, and moved towards her, but she backed away and sat down rather abruptly on the sofa.

'As it happened,' she said acidly, 'I frightened the intruders, not the other way round. They thought I was a ghost.'

'The way you look now I can see why!' Alex sat down beside her and seized her hands. 'Sarah—promise me you'll never do anything like that again!'

She gritted her teeth as his grip hurt her wrist. 'Oh, I won't. Looking back on it in the light of day, I can't believe I was so stupid! But Jack's away and Tim had gone off for the night to take his family to Wiltshire, so I couldn't just stand by and let the vandals get away before the police came.'

'No,' he said heavily. 'You couldn't let anything happen to your beloved house.'

Sarah decided to ignore that. 'Anyway, they were the merest amateurs—young lads, not experienced criminals. The truck they had was useless for making away with heavy stone objects—which is why it overturned when they panicked. They hadn't loaded it properly.'

'I'm thankful they didn't overturn it on top of you—'

'Why, exactly, should *you* be thankful?' said Sarah swiftly.

Alex looked at her in silence, his eyes inscrutable. Then he released her hands and moved away a little. 'I would care if any employee of the consortium were run over by a truck, of course. What other reason could I have?'

Sarah bit her lip and looked away. 'It was very kind of you to come down here to see me.'

'Yes, it was, wasn't it,' he said with sarcasm, 'when you consider the reception I get whenever I come within yards of you? At least this time you had a woman with you when I barged in.'

'If you're referring to Martin—'

'You know damn well I am!'

'He came down that day to invite me to a party.'

Alex eyed her morosely. 'No telephone in his house?'

'Isobel suggested he escaped from the joys of fatherhood for an afternoon and came to ask me in person,' said Sarah loftily.

Alex shrugged in disbelief. 'You're on remarkably good terms with a man who dumped you for another woman.'

She glared at him. 'Martin and I, Isobel too, are civilised adults. He still cares about me, and I'm still fond of him. We're good friends—'

'I could never be satisfied with that!'

Her eyes narrowed. 'With what?'

'Having been your lover—brief though the experience was—I could never settle for anything less, Sarah.' He saw her swallow drily and his eyes lit with remembered, pulse-quickening heat. 'From the moment I first saw you I knew how it would be between us. And don't try to deny you feel the same way, because you do. Why won't you give in and admit it?'

'Have you forgotten Felicity?' she demanded.

'I can explain all that,' he said impatiently, but Sarah held up her hand.

'No need. In your life there'll always be a Felicity.'

'Sarah, for God's sake listen to me,' he said with sudden passion. 'I'm in love with you; I want to share your life and I want you to share mine. Felicity was here because—'

'You needed to show me that my rejection didn't matter,' she finished for him.

All the heat and passion drained from his face as Alex stared at her in silence for so long that she became restive. 'Ah. So that's it,' he said softly at last. 'Now I understand.'

Sarah stiffened. 'Understand what?'

'It's nothing to do with Felicity, is it? In fact, Sarah, you sent me packing before you ever laid eyes on her.' Alex rose to his feet, looking down at her. 'Because I've never had a long-standing relationship with a woman you automatically assume I'm incapable of one in the future.' His eyes bored into hers. 'You keep up the friendship with Dryden because you're too proud to admit he hurt you. And you won't let yourself get close to me because you're convinced that some day I'd dish out the same treatment he did.'

Sarah jumped to her feet, her eyes flashing angrily. 'I object to the amateur psychology! But you're right on one point. I do doubt your capacity for commitment—it was confirmed by someone in a position to know.'

'Who?' he demanded.

'Your mother.' Sarah smiled in triumph. 'She told me herself that one word about settling down and you run a mile.'

Alex's face set in grim lines. 'In that case there's no more to be said. Who am I to contradict my mother?' He glanced at his watch. 'I must go. My parents will be relieved to know you're more or less in one piece.'

'Thank them for their concern,' said Sarah distantly. 'My thanks to you, too. It was very good of you to come all this way.'

Alex shrugged. 'It was one of my famous impulses again. I had some chivalrous notion about offering to sleep here for a while so that you could go to your parents to recover.'

'How very kind, but it's quite unnecessary. I'll be back to normal tomorrow.'

'In short,' he said bitterly, 'you want nothing from me.'

Oh, but I do, thought Sarah with longing.

Alex moved swiftly and caught her in his arms. 'Whether you do or not I want this,' he muttered against her mouth, and kissed her savagely. She tried to push him away, but her sprained wrist protested, and she gave up the struggle. He raised his head at last, his eyes glittering as they stared into hers. 'Trust me, Sarah.'

'What do you mean?' she said huskily. 'What is it you want from me?'

'Everything you've got to give!'

'Let's sit down,' she said, surprising him, and he sat close beside her on the sofa, gazing at her in remorse.

'I'm sorry. I shouldn't have been so rough.'

'I'm not quite myself yet,' she admitted, trying to smile.

'Somehow I don't think we'd be having this conversation if you were!'

'You wouldn't be here at all if I hadn't been so reckless last night,' she pointed out.

Alex smiled and reached for her hand, smoothing the back of it with one finger in a familiar caress. 'I wouldn't be so sure. If you must know, Sarah, I intended coming here today anyway.'

'Why? You didn't come to the concert last week,' she retorted, then could have kicked herself at the look of triumph in his eyes.

'You missed me,' he said gloatingly.

'I just wondered if you'd be there, that's all,' she muttered, looking away.

'My mother said you looked very beautiful—made rather a point of it when I arrived back from Germany yesterday.' His mouth twisted. 'You feature in her conversation quite a lot.'

Sarah looked down at the hand holding hers. 'Alex, let's put our cards on the table. You say you're in love with me—'

'I'm not just saying it—I am! What does it take to convince you?' He turned her face up to his. 'Tell me the truth. How do you feel about me?'

'The same,' she said simply, and he closed his eyes for a second, then caught her to him. 'Wait!' she said breathlessly.

'I don't want to wait,' he said against her mouth. 'I want to take you to bed and keep you there—'

'But you can't. Not here,' she said urgently, and Alex drew back, his eyes narrowed as he stared down at her.

'What are you saying, Sarah?'

She drew in a deep breath. 'If I'd met you somewhere else it would have been different almost from the start. If I'd had a different kind of job, with a flat in London like you, it would have been simple. We could have been together in either place as much as we liked, without an interested audience following every move. Which would be inevitable here.'

Alex's jaw tightened. 'I don't know where this is leading.'

Sarah looked at him in appeal. 'I'm trying to say that I've given in. To myself as well as you. If you want us to be lovers I will, because I can't go on pretending it's not what I want too. But not here. I'll come up to your place in London as often as I can. That way, if—when— the arrangement comes to an end no one here need know. I can carry on with my job and you can—'

'Go off and find myself another Felicity, I suppose,' said Alex bitingly. 'As you're obviously convinced I will.' He jumped to his feet. 'Oh, no, Sarah. We've got our wires crossed somewhere. Ravishing though the occasional session in bed would be—when you could spare the time to tear yourself away from this place, of course—I regret I must refuse. My idea of a viable relationship is vastly different.'

Sarah stared up at Alex in dismay, her heart sinking at the bleak, withdrawn look on his face. 'Then tell me what you want!'

'I thought I had,' he said with sudden violence. 'But since you so obviously weren't listening I'm going, before I say something I'll regret.'

'Alex!' Sarah jumped to her feet, then grabbed the arm of a chair, feeling giddy, suddenly reminded that she'd had a recent knock on the head.

Alex caught her by the elbows, steadying her. 'You'd be better off in bed! Alone,' he added wearily, 'just in case I'm not making myself clear again. Is there anything I can do for you before I go?'

'No,' said Sarah, clutching at the torn remnants of her pride. 'Absolutely nothing. You're right. I think I will go to bed. I need to be fit for tomorrow. I'm due at the house.'

Alex said something short and pithy about the house, and went to the door. 'I'll see myself out,' he said formally. 'I hope you feel better soon. Goodbye, Sarah.'

CHAPTER ELEVEN

SARAH'S adventure was the entire topic of conversation in the house for a day or two, but the general interest faded eventually, along with the bruise which made dark glasses a necessary fashion accessory for a while. Sarah was glad of their cover as she moved through the days like an automaton, utterly mortified that she'd offered herself to Alex Mackenzie only to be refused. Had he really expected to move in here with her in the house? Sarah shuddered at the thought.

'Look, Sarah,' said Liz one morning as she watched Sarah clean the heavy silver candlesticks from the drawing-room, 'you haven't been the same since that night. Are you unhappy about sleeping in the flat alone? Jack thinks you're nervous after what happened.'

'He's wrong, Liz. I'm not. I just suffered a bit with reaction for a few days, that's all.' Sarah smiled reassuringly, but Liz looked unconvinced.

'I heard Alex Mackenzie came down to see you.'

'Yes, he did. His parents were worried when they heard, so he came to see if I was all in one piece. Actually,' added Sarah, trying to be fair, 'he came to offer to sleep in the house for a few days so I could go home to my parents.'

Liz stared at her, exasperated. 'Then why on earth didn't you?'

Sarah fitted the various parts of the candelabra back together with care, frowning in concentration. 'I thought it best to stay put. You know, like getting back on a horse after being thrown. It worked. No nerves, I promise.'

'Good thing you're off for the weekend, anyway,' said Liz. 'Where are you going?'

'London—to a party. My sister's putting me up.'

'About time you let your hair down for a bit, Sarah! Are you wearing that gorgeous brown dress?'

'No.' Sarah blenched at the thought. 'Jane's lending me one of hers. Too tight round her hips, apparently, since her holiday.'

Jack came in to interrupt them. 'I just had a call from a gentleman who couldn't reach you on your mobile, Sarah.'

Sarah's heart leapt in her chest as she reached for the telephone. 'I've had it switched off all this time,' she said, pulling a face. 'Who was it, Jack?'

'A Mr Ben Ferris. Wants you to call back.'

'OK,' said Sarah casually, 'I'll ring him when we've finished these.' She'd known it wasn't Alex, of course, because Jack would have said. But she'd hoped.

Ben, when she finally called him, was voluble with contrition. 'Would you mind terribly, Sarah, if I cancelled for tomorrow night?'

'Of course not. You're not ill, I hope?'

'No, love.' He paused. 'The thing is, Sarah, I've met this most wonderful girl. She started with the firm last week, and—well, to be mushy, I took one look at her and thought, This is it. This is the one—the whole bag—wedding ring, babies, the lot! Laura's asked me round to her place for dinner tomorrow night and—'

'And you didn't fancy telling her you were taking another woman to a party!' Sarah laughed, gave him her blessing, assured him that she could perfectly well go to the Drydens' on her own, and rang off, feeling rather deflated.

Ben had been around at intervals for years, since they were students, the last one of their particular circle to evade a long-term relationship. Sarah sighed. If he was all set to embark on one at last she would miss the occasional night on the town with him.

By the time Sarah was ready for the party Jane had already departed for the evening, having assured her sister she looked drop-dead gorgeous. The borrowed sleeveless dress consisted of two layers of bias-cut, knee-skimming silk chiffon in a shade somewhere between cream and pink, and, as Jane had promised, it gave Sarah's skin a glow, and looked prefect against the fiery hair she'd been coaxed to leave loose.

'Gosh, you look ravishing,' said Isobel Dryden when she let Sarah in. 'And to think that at one time I was thinner than you!'

Isobel, it was true, was very different from the slender, ethereal creature who'd captured Martin Dryden's heart. These days, after the birth of her children, and a life-style which involved sitting down at a computer for long periods at a time, Isobel's figure was more earth mother than wood nymph. But her wild cascade of dark ringlets and huge green eyes were still as arresting as ever, her success as a novelist had given her self-confidence, and the increased opulence of her curves, she confided to Sarah, was not due entirely to the little Drydens she'd already produced, but to the future arrival of another.

'We asked you early to give you the glad news,' said Martin, kissing Sarah. 'We have time for a celebration glass of bubbly before the rest arrive.' He led her into the large room the Drydens used only on formal occasions. 'So far we've managed to keep this one part of the house free from the vandalism of our little darlings.'

'I rather hoped I might see Jamie and the twins.' Sarah smiled cajolingly. 'Can I go up and have a peep?'

Isobel shuddered. 'Not in that dress. Could you pop up later when Dinah's got them off to sleep? Otherwise Jamie will be clamouring to come down and join in the fun. We've had words about it already.'

Sarah laughed. 'I'll be good, then. By the way, Ben's deserted me for another woman at last,' she added flippantly.

'Amazing he hasn't long since, really,' said Isobel, who knew Ben from her student days. 'He's hankered after you so long, Sarah, it's time he either cut loose or bullied you into marrying him.'

'There was never any question of that!' protested Sarah.

'Not on your side, maybe,' said Martin drily. 'On young Ferris's part the feelings were never quite so platonic, I fancy.'

The thought raised Sarah's spirits a notch as the other guests began to arrive. And since the great majority of those present were writers or actors, or in some form of entertainment, she began to enjoy herself enormously, either Martin or Isobel, perfect hosts as always, introducing her to people they knew would interest her. Sarah met the actress due to star in the television series, renewed her acquaintance with some old friends of Martin's and ate the delicious catered supper in company with one of them. Max Lawson lectured in medieval history, and professed himself totally fascinated by

Sarah's job. He was an interesting man, and made it gratifyingly plain that he found her attractive as he drew her out on her role at Ingham Lacey, begging a personal conducted tour if he visited there one day.

Sarah responded easily to the form of wry, sardonic flirtation that Max Lawson indulged in, and after supper promised to rejoin him after making some repairs to her face.

'What I really want is a peep at the little darlings,' she said to Isobel at the foot of the stairs.

'Yes, of course. You can use their bathroom on the top floor before you look in on them—but just peeping, Sarah. I beg you!'

The plea was in vain. When Sarah looked in on Jamie, she found him sitting up in his bed, surrounded by books and puzzles, a selection of bears crowded in alongside him.

'Aunty Sarah!' he said, brightening. 'Mummy says I can't come down. Will you read to me?'

'Of course I will.' Sarah slid off her shoes and settled herself on the bed beside him. 'Right, then, Jamie Dryden, tell me which stories you want, then snuggle down while I read.'

The little boy made his choice, then the flaxen head burrowed into the pillow obediently as Sarah began on *The Tale of Jemima Puddle-Duck*. Eyes drooping, Jamie demanded *Babar the Elephant* as an encore, and, though he struggled to stay awake, by the end of the story he was fast asleep.

Sarah picked up her shoes and stole quietly from the room to visit the twins next door. The little girls were fast asleep, to her relief, looking like a pair of cherubs in their cots, their flushed identical faces so angelic that

Sarah felt a pain somewhere in her midriff at the sight of them.

She backed from the room onto the landing, paused to slide her feet into her shoes, then smothered a cry of disbelief as she straightened to find herself face to face with Alex Mackenzie. Sarah closed her eyes for a moment, certain she was dreaming, but when she opened them he was still there, dressed in one of his impeccable suits, his face inscrutable in the dim light of the attic landing, too immovable a presence to be a figment of her imagination.

Sarah put a finger to her lips and led the way down to the next floor. The landings in the Dryden house were large, pleasant spaces, and this one had a sofa and a console table, with a rose-shaded lamp to provide a pleasantly muted light.

'Sit here for a moment,' said Alex, and Sarah was glad to, decidedly weak at the knees at finding him in such an unlikely place.

'Mrs Dryden said you'd gone up to look at the children, and that if I promised on my honour not to wake them I should follow you,' he said, sitting beside her.

Sarah raised an eyebrow at him, fast recovering from the surprise. 'Which explains your presence on the top-floor landing but not how you come to be here at the party. I assume,' she added, 'that you were invited?'

'I was. I haven't gatecrashed a party since I was eighteen.' He looked at her in silence, subjecting her to such a long, slow scrutiny from head to foot that Sarah had to exert her will-power to keep still. 'Mrs Dryden sent me an invitation in the usual way.'

'Odd you never thought to mention it last time we met.' Her eyes met his challengingly.

'I had other things on my mind,' he said expressionlessly. 'Besides, if I had you wouldn't have come.'

'Wouldn't you have preferred that?' she parried. 'You weren't exactly pleased with me when you took off that day.'

'No. Which doesn't make it easier.'

'Make what easier?'

'Being away from you,' he said grudgingly.

'It's your choice!'

'No, it's not my choice, dammit, Sarah.' Alex controlled himself with effort as some female guests came up to visit the nearby bathroom. 'This isn't the ideal place for private conversation,' he said irritably.

'You were the one who turned my suggestion down,' hissed Sarah in a fierce undertone.

'Do you wonder?' He glared at her. 'It was an insult!'

Her eyes flashed at him dangerously. 'It's not an insult I've offered to anyone else—nor ever will again!'

'Just as well. Only a fool would accept.' He folded his arms and stared down at his shoes malevolently. 'Where you're concerned I've been a fool all along. No doubt your professor agrees.'

'Why should he?'

'He saw the painting.' He shot a cold look at her. 'You told him I did it?'

'Yes,' she snapped, her look equally glacial. 'Are you ashamed of it?'

'No.' His mouth twisted. 'But depicting you as an angel was a serious error of judgement on my part.'

'Confirmed, of course, when I offered to be your bit on the side!'

Alex turned on her in fury, looking as though he wanted to shake the living daylights out of her. 'The description's yours, not mine—' He turned away, struggling to keep his anger in check as the occupants of the bathroom emerged again, casting curious looks in their direction as they went downstairs. Martin Dryden exchanged pleasantries with them as he came past them with a bottle in one hand, two glasses in the other. He smiled at Sarah in wry apology as he put them down on the table, then turned to Alex, who'd risen at his approach.

'I gather you came by cab, Mackenzie, so if you're not driving home please indulge as much as you like.'

'Thank you,' said Alex stiffly. 'You're very kind. I came straight from the station.'

'Plenty of food downstairs. Please help yourself,' said Martin, well aware of the constraint in the atmosphere.

'I ate on the train,' said Alex, and forced a smile. 'I gather you're celebrating your wife's success.'

'In more ways than one,' said Martin blandly. 'Sarah will explain—must get back to the revels.' He smiled at a conspicuously silent Sarah, and went back down the stairs.

'What did he mean?' said Alex, filling the glass.

'Isobel's expecting another baby.'

'How many do they have?'

'Three. Jamie and the twins, Alice and Rose.'

He drank the wine down almost in one draught. 'Isobel Dryden's production rate is spectacular.'

'Martin's fifty, remember. He can hardly hang about.'

'And Isobel?'

'A year younger than me.' Sarah sipped the champagne absent-mindedly. 'She was a first year when I was doing my finals. Had glandular fever and took a year out before taking up her university place. She looked like a piece of thistledown in those days.'

'Do I detect a note of satisfaction?'

Sarah turned glittering dark eyes on him. 'You bet your life you do. I'm only human.'

'So am I,' he said bitterly, staring down into his glass. 'Otherwise I wouldn't have come running here tonight just on the off chance of seeing you.'

'Did you?' she asked very quietly.

'You know damn well I did. Besides,' he added, turning to look at her, 'I was curious to visit the Dryden household, to view this adult, civilised threesome of yours at first hand. Frankly, I prefer the lady of the house to her husband.'

'Men always take to Isobel.'

'And you resent that?'

'Not any more. I'm fond of her, strange as it may seem. I'm very pleased Isobel's so successful as a novelist. And I adore her children.' Sarah gave him a wry smile. 'But if motherhood had left her skinny and waif-like as well it would have been too much—even for a civilised adult like me.' She frowned suddenly. 'How did she get in contact with you, by the way? Mutual acquaintances?'

'No. She rang me at the office, explained who she was and asked me to the party. Your presence was offered as the incentive to accept.'

Sarah gave an inelegant snort. 'I'm surprised you didn't turn her down flat at the mention of my name.'

Alex turned on her, his eyes holding hers. 'In actual fact I thanked her very politely and said I'd be delighted. I intended to be here earlier, but I missed the earlier train. I've been in Scotland all week, otherwise I'd have been in touch before.'

'Why?' she asked bluntly.

'Because I need to talk to you—yet now I'm here, face to face with you at last, I realise there's something I must do before any real talking's possible,' he said cryptically, and offered her more champagne.

Sarah shook her head, half expecting him to seize her in his arms and kiss her senseless, regardless of any guests who might come wandering up the stairs. But this, it seemed, was not what Alex meant by the prologue to discussion.

'Are you on duty at Ingham Lacey tomorrow?' he asked, after an interval in which Sarah had seriously contemplated throwing herself in his arms and assuring him that no more talk was necessary.

'Yes,' she said tensely, hoping this meant he wanted her to take the day off and spend it with him.

'Have tea with me once the crowds begin to subside,' he said.

'Very well,' she responded, mystified. Tea? She wanted a lot more than that. She choked back a laugh, and he shot a bright, questioning look at her.

'Something funny, Sarah?'

'Funny peculiar, rather,' she assured him, and stood up, the borrowed chiffon drifting about her as Alex jumped to his feet. 'Perhaps we should join the party. Isobel always invites interesting people.' She smiled up at him through her lashes. 'None of them quite as dramatic a surprise as you, admittedly.'

He smiled back, his eyes alight with the familiar gleam. 'Did you think I was an apparition when you found me upstairs?'

She nodded ruefully. 'It was only a strong desire to let sleeping babies lie that kept me from screaming. Ned Frome couldn't have shocked me more.'

'To quote someone,' he said, taking her hand, 'I'm flesh and blood, Sarah.'

She breathed deeply. 'So you are.'

Their eyes held.

'I was watching you upstairs,' he said huskily. 'While you were reading to the little boy.'

'Did you enjoy *Jemima Puddle-Duck*?'

'You were halfway through *Babar* by the time I tracked you down.' His grasp tightened. 'He's a lucky lad.'

'Jamie?'

Alex nodded. 'I don't sleep very well these days— perhaps a bedtime story might do the trick.'

Sarah tore her eyes from his. 'Time we went down. I'll introduce you to people.'

'I came to see you, Sarah, but,' he added with a sigh, 'I shall play the polite guest, if only out of gratitude to Mrs Dryden.'

'Which reminds me,' said Sarah as they went downstairs, 'I must ask Isobel why she took it in her head to invite you.'

But Sarah had no opportunity for private conversation. The moment Isobel spotted them she took them on a tour of the room. Alex exchanged pleasantries obediently, but with his arm around Sarah's waist in a way which made it very obvious to all comers that she was the reason for his presence, also that he had no intention of separating from her—not even when two of the guests would have liked him to linger. Sarah found herself the subject of sharp scrutiny from two of the most beautiful women in the room, one of them a fashion editor, the other the wife of Isobel's agent, and both, it seemed, were old friends of Alex Mackenzie's.

But Alex, as he made quite plain, was in no mood for auld lang syne. He introduced Sarah, exchanged small talk for a while, then led her away to bid their hosts goodnight.

'Thank you for inviting me, Mrs Dryden.' He smiled at Isobel with such warmth that she looked at Sarah with a gleam of smug triumph as Alex went to take his leave of Martin.

'Surprised?' she murmured.

'Yes.'

'I meddled. But I'm not sorry. Blame it on my penchant for happy endings, both fiction and fact.'

'You're a bit previous there, Isobel,' said Sarah drily.

'Want to bet?' Isobel turned her smile on Alex as he rejoined them with Martin. 'I'm so glad you could make it, Mr Mackenzie.'

'So am I,' he said simply, with a look at Sarah.

'You must come and see us again—dinner, perhaps,' said Martin affably.

'Thank you,' said Alex, looking round as the doorbell rang. 'I rather think that's my cab. I asked him to come back. Do you have a coat, Sarah?'

She eyed him narrowly. 'Am I coming with you, then?'

'You most certainly are,' he said flatly, tempering it with a smile at the Drydens.

Sarah shrugged, smiling at Isobel and Martin. 'It seems I'm homeward bound, willy-nilly. Thank you both. Your parties are always brilliant, Isobel—this one was no exception.'

'We aim to please,' said Martin drily. 'Goodnight to you both. Safe journey.'

When they were outside Sarah gazed up at her companion challengingly. 'That was very high-handed, Alex Mackenzie. I might not have wanted to leave the party—and I could be going back to Ingham Lacey tonight for all you know.'

'Isobel told me you were staying in Bayswater,' said Alex matter-of-factly, ushering her into the taxi. 'I'll drop you off there on my way. What's the address?'

Deciding it was a bit late in the day to make a fuss, Sarah told him, then said nothing more for a long time because once the cab began to move Alex took her in his arms and put an end to conversation with a kiss which silenced her very effectively. The kiss went on and on until their hearts were hammering and Sarah thought she'd suffocate, and didn't care a jot if she did just as long as Alex went on kissing her. When he raised his head at last he looked down into her dazed eyes for a long time, then sat back in the seat, holding her cradled against his shoulder, in smouldering silence, his hand smoothing her hair as their breathing slowed.

When they arrived near the familiar pillared portico Alex asked the taxi driver to wait, then saw Sarah into the house and down into the basement to Jane's front door. Still in silence, Alex watched as Sarah unlocked the door, then he took her in his arms and kissed her again, in a manner which said more than any declaration of intent might have done. When he released her he smiled down into her eyes, trailing a hand down her cheek.

'Tomorrow!'

Sarah was up at the crack of dawn. She left a note for her sleeping sister, and drove to Kent through warm, silvery drizzle which did nothing to dampen her mood. Today, she vowed as she left the motorway, she would come to some kind of agreement with Alex Mackenzie or die in the attempt. Life was too short to waste it languishing over past regrets—or future ones.

Mid-afternoon, as though conscious of what was expected, the sun came out and Ingham Lacey basked in its beauty as the crowds thinned out and the hands of the stable clock moved towards four. Sarah tried not to watch it, and kept scrupulously to the usual routine of the day as she visited each room in turn to see that all was running smoothly in her domain.

'Liz wants to know if you enjoyed the party,' said Jack Wells at one point, and grinned. 'Not that I need to ask. You obviously did, by the sparkle about you.'

'Why, Jack, how nice of you to notice,' mocked Sarah. 'And tell Liz the party was great fun. I had a wonderful time.'

Sarah was leaving the shop, after a discussion on re-ordering, when she saw Alex coming towards her with his usual purposeful stride. Sarah gave him a radiant smile of welcome, but it faded abruptly as she realised he wasn't alone. Two young women and a tall, fair boy were following close behind. And the younger of the women was Felicity.

'Sarah!' Alex grasped her firmly by the hand. 'I'd like you to meet my sister, Iona.'

Sarah managed to summon a smile, holding out her free hand, and Alex's sister, blonde and pretty like her mother, shook it with enthusiasm, her eyes twinkling as her brother resisted Sarah's attempts to free herself.

'My mother's talked about you such a lot, but I don't get down to this part of the world much these days, so I haven't been to see for myself.'

See what for herself? thought Sarah.

Felicity eyed her diffidently. 'Hello, Sarah, how are you?'

Sarah smiled brightly. 'Well, but busy, as usual.'

'I heard about your adventure.' Felicity shuddered. 'I don't know how you could be so brave.'

'I wouldn't call it brave,' said Alex darkly. 'This is Harry Warner, by the way. Harry, this is Miss Sarah Law, who rules this place with a rod of iron.'

Sarah contained herself with difficulty and gave the boy a warm smile. 'Hello, Harry. Actually Colonel Newby runs the place. I'm the housekeeper.'

Harry shook her hand, grinning. 'Crikey, are you really?'

'People tend to find it hard to believe.' Alex looked towards the restaurant. 'Is it still crowded out in there, Sarah?'

She detached her hand firmly. 'I've got tea waiting in the flat,' she informed him, in no mood to take tea in the restaurant with Felicity as one of the party. She looked at Alex's sister. 'If you come with me across the courtyard and through the gatehouse, you'll see a "Private" notice at the foot of the spiral stairs. My rooms are at the top.'

Once in her own quarters Sarah felt marginally better. She showed her guests into the sitting-room, flatly refused Alex's offer of help, and rejoined the others in only the time it took to make tea and add the necessary china to the tray. Alex jumped to his feet to take the tray from her.

'Thank you,' said Sarah evenly. 'If you'd put it on the table under the window, perhaps Felicity would distribute cups as I pour. Oh, by the way,' she said to the girl as Felicity sprang eagerly to help, 'on the kitchen counter you'll find a plate of cakes from the tea-shop. Would you mind? You know the way, of course,' she added, with a look at Alex.

'This is a lovely room,' said Iona, looking round. 'The view alone is fabulous. Those cottages are so picturesque.'

'I used to live in one of them,' said Sarah, pouring tea.

'Wouldn't you prefer that?' said the other woman curiously. 'It must be creepy here alone at night.'

'Fliss says the place is haunted,' said Harry with relish. 'Have you ever seen the ghost, Miss Law?'

'No. Not that I'd let him chase me out. I love it here.' Sarah looked up with a smile as Felicity returned with the cakes. 'Thank you. Would you hand them round?'

'Did you know it was haunted before you stayed here, Fliss?' asked Harry, taking an éclair.

'No fear.' She pulled a face. 'Otherwise nothing would have made me stay here. Even as it was, Alex was such a crosspatch I was glad to get away.'

'You nearly burned the place down,' he reminded her.

'Don't remind me!' Felicity shuddered and threw herself down beside Harry. 'I die with embarrassment every time I think of it.'

He laughed uproariously and put his arm round her, pulling her close. 'I wish I'd been here!'

Sarah eyed them blankly.

'Could I have some tea?' asked Alex in her ear.

'Yes—yes, of course.' Sarah poured it hastily, and he took the cup from her and sat beside her.

'It's a wonder Alex didn't spank you,' said Iona. 'He's given me a hiding in the past for far less.'

'Rubbish,' said Alex promptly. 'I gave you a few taps on the behind once when I was a student. She meddled with my computer,' he explained to the others, 'and lost part of my dissertation for me.'

Iona pulled a face. 'I thought I'd never hear the end of that one. My parents even sided with him—said I deserved it.'

Felicity sat up straight in awe. 'Iona *Morton*! What a thing to do. Weren't you scared when he found out?'

Morton? thought Sarah.

'Petrified,' said Iona with feeling. 'Though my behind was anything but when Alex had done with me. You can make it up to me now,' she added to her brother, holding up her cup. 'I'd like more tea.'

'Anyway,' said Felicity, eyeing Alex blackly, 'never ask your darling brother to pick me up from school again. He was an absolute pig to me—'

'Can you blame him?' demanded Iona. 'You nearly burnt down five centuries of history!'

'I *didn't*! I was only trying to be helpful by cooking some steaks. I didn't know I was going to set off the entire alarm system.'

'You do realise that it was well into the small hours before Sarah got everything safely back,' said Alex sternly.

'Of course I know,' said Felicity with contrition. 'I felt awful about it, really I did. I wanted to come and help, Sarah—stop laughing, Harry.'

'I can't,' crowed the boy. 'I just wish I'd been here—preferably with a video camera!'

'It was very good fire practice,' said Sarah soothingly, the mention of the solitary word 'school' acting like adrenaline in her blood. 'We managed to get most of the valuables out in record time, furniture included.'

'Dear, oh, dear,' said Iona in remorse. 'I didn't know what I was letting you in for when I asked Alex to collect Fliss that day.'

'No,' said Alex, staring into his cup. 'You certainly didn't.'

His sister eyed him narrowly. 'I couldn't help the children's measles!'

'My parents are lecturers,' explained Fliss to Sarah. 'They were both away at the same conference, which overlapped my exeat weekend by a day. Iona was supposed to collect me and take me home to stay with her and my brother for the night.' She scowled at Alex. 'But measles struck, so Alex was roped in. Never again.'

'Amen to that,' said Alex with emphasis.

'I volunteered for the job,' said Harry glumly, 'but Mrs Morton declined the offer.'

'I can just see Dr Withers, the headmistress, if my boyfriend turned up to collect me from school,' hooted Felicity. 'Her girls are expected to be pure.'

'At your age I should damn well hope so,' said Alex, grinning.

'Get real, Alex Mackenzie—I'm seventeen years old, not seven!'

Whilst this good-humoured banter was in progress Sarah was busy absorbing the information Felicity had imparted. So Felicity and Iona were sisters-in-law... Everything was suddenly falling into place...

Sarah jumped up, feeling strangely light-headed. 'Shall I make more tea, or shall we have something stronger?'

'Are we celebrating something?' enquired Alex, getting up. Ignoring the blatant interest of the others, he took her hand.

'I hope we are,' she said deliberately, at which point Iona stood up and gestured to the other two.

'Come on, let's away.' She smiled at Sarah. 'I'm so glad to meet you at last. Thanks for the tea. Alex roped me in to bring these two today, so I left the boys with Mother, but bathtime approaches.'

Alex kissed her cheek. 'Thanks. I owe you.'

Felicity smiled shyly at Sarah. 'It was lovely to see you again.'

'It was lovely to see you too,' said Sarah with complete truth. She ruffled the girl's pale hair and shook Harry's hand, then looked at Iona.

'Perhaps you'll come back another time, when the house is closed?'

Iona smiled warmly. 'I'd love to.'

When they were alone Alex looked at Sarah, eyebrows raised. 'You haven't asked why I'm not driving back with them. Does that mean you're willing to give me a bed for the night?'

'No,' she said with composure, stacking china on the tray. 'I assumed you'd driven down separately.'

He seized her in his arms suddenly. 'Stop looking so serene and unruffled, woman!'

'The quickest way to ruffle me,' she flung at him, 'is to call me "woman"!'

Alex laughed and held her close. 'Then what shall I say? Miss Law? My darling?'

She nodded, rubbing her cheek against his. 'Mmm.'

'Is there any need for more talking?' he asked, holding her away from him.

Sarah looked up at him, one eyebrow raised. 'Why didn't you explain about Felicity before?'

'If you remember, I tried on several occasions,' he pointed out. 'You flatly refused to listen. Nor is Felicity relevant. Your rejection came prior to any knowledge of the girl's existence.'

'Yes,' she agreed quietly. 'I know.'

'Leave the tray,' he ordered, and sat down on the sofa, drawing her down with him to sit on his lap. He held her close, her hair spilling like fire against the white of his shirt as she burrowed against his shoulder. 'Now tell me why, Sarah. I need to know.'

'You know already. It was you who told me, in fact— the day you more or less accused me of cowardice when it came to risking more rejection. And you were right.' Sarah lifted her head to look up at him. 'Your reputation preceded you here, Alex. You were well known for being not only an eligible bachelor, but one very determined to remain that way. Something your mother confirmed the night of the party. By that time I was already so hopelessly in love with you I couldn't resist temptation that night. But the whole experience was so— so glorious, like nothing I'd known before, that I decided to end it sooner rather than later, before my heart got chewed up in pieces.'

Alex breathed in deeply as he stared down at her. 'My mother was only saying what everyone knew was true— up to the moment I met you. How could she know she was scaring off the one woman in my life I wanted to keep there for good?'

'Do you?'

'Want you for keeps?' He laughed unsteadily. 'What else can I do to convince you? I told you I wasn't the type to beg—'

Sarah put a hand to his lips. 'And you don't have to. Because I want it too. On your terms.'

'What terms?' he asked, frowning. 'I haven't made any.'

She looked blank. 'Well, I suppose I don't know, really. I thought you'd want us to be together. Live together and so on.'

'People usually do if they love each other,' he pointed out. 'Do you love me, Sarah?'

'Yes.' She brought his head down and kissed him fiercely. 'I love you to bits, if you want the details—'

'I do.' He returned the kiss with interest. 'You're all I think about, all I've ever wanted. Why else do you think I keep coming back here like a lovesick schoolboy, why I played that stupid trick with Felicity just to make you jealous?' He let out a bark of mirthless laughter. 'She was in her uniform when I collected her from school—hideous cotton dress, blazer, straw boater, et cetera. We stopped at a pub for lunch and she begged to change her clothes.' He shook his head. 'I think of Fliss as a little girl—my jaw dropped when she reappeared in skin-tight jeans and vest-top. Talk about jailbait! That was when I had the brilliant idea of bringing her here for the night instead of delivering her to my parents.'

'You utter swine!' Sarah bounced up, glaring at him. 'One look at her was like a punch in the stomach! I was so jealous I was hard put to be polite.'

'I hoped you were,' he said, and kissed her hungrily. 'I wanted you to be jealous,' he muttered against her lips. 'I wanted to hurt you the way you hurt me when you told me to get lost. Then I couldn't stand being away from you and came chasing down here, only to find you with Dryden.'

'Your face was a picture,' she gloated. 'I thought you were going to hit him.'

'For a split-second so did I.' He shook her slightly. 'I do not like your professor, Sarah Law. His wife wasn't playing fairy godmother to you, Sarah, by getting me to the party. She wants you safely tied up to someone else, to scotch the *tendre* her husband still harbours for you, the bastard.'

'If you dislike him that much why did you accept the invitation to the party last night?' she demanded, deeply pleased by his jealousy.

'Why does a drowning man clutch at a spar?' he countered. 'If it meant seeing you I wasn't going to refuse.'

'And if you hadn't been invited, what then?'

'I would have come down here today just as I have done, complete with my sister and Felicity. I hadn't bargained for Harry as well, but these days they come as a pair, apparently, and it was worth bringing him just to see your face when they were curled up on this very sofa together.' Alex smiled down into her face. 'But never mind all that; tell me again that you love me.'

Sarah complied with such fervour that it was some time later before Alex pushed her away and sat in the far corner of the sofa, breathing heavily.

'Let's talk.'

'No,' she said, edging nearer. 'Let's go to bed.'

He closed his eyes as if in mortal anguish. 'Don't! We haven't discussed these mythical terms of mine. Or you could outline some of your own. Whichever.'

'Last time I suggested something,' she reminded him, eyes flashing, 'you threw it out of court.'

His eyes opened, kindling. 'Ah, yes. A night of passion now and then when our diaries had a matching window.'

Sarah bit her lip. 'All right, then, Mackenzie. You talk terms.'

'Pretty basic, really. I thought I'd come and live here just as I originally planned—only with you instead of alone. And not here in the house.'

'But that leaves the original problem unsolved,' she said, frowning.

'No. We're taking on an assistant administrator to help Colonel Newby with the estate, because my father's acquired more land. The new man's a bachelor, and perfectly happy to live here in the private quarters.'

'So where am I to live?' demanded Sarah.

'With me.'

'That part we've settled,' she said impatiently. 'I just want to know where.'

Alex smiled. 'The owner of this land Dad's bought has sold his house along with it. It's by the river at Hopford—'

'You mean Mill House?' Sarah's eyes widened. 'I've been there once or twice to charity lunches. It's a heavenly house.'

'It's ours if we want it. By which I take it that one problem's solved?' Alex moved back to take her in his arms. He looked down into her flushed face. 'But let's clear up a few other details. First I want to make it clear that I'm discussing a partnership for life. If you don't fancy the idea of marriage I can live with that. If you do I can live with that even more happily. But, my darling, rejection on either side, is never, ever going to be part of the deal. You, Sarah, are the other part of me I've been looking for all my life. I'll never give you up. So before you say yes to anything I want you to think about that very carefully. I mean it.'

Sarah pretended to think. She looked up at him at last, her heart in her eyes. 'I think I can live with that,' she mimicked hoarsely, the last words muffled when he seized her to him and kissed her until her head was reeling.

He picked her up. 'Did I mention that a very important part of this relationship involves making love a lot?'

'No,' she whispered as he carried her along the hall. 'But I thought it might. I think it's *such* a good idea.'

'Good. I do too,' he panted, and they collapsed together on the bed in the larger bedroom. 'In fact, right now I think I should warn you that if we don't make love in about another second or so I'm likely to go up in smoke.'

'Don't do that!' she said as they threw their clothes off. 'The alarms will go off!'

They laughed helplessly, holding each other close, then the laughter died, replaced by heat and passion and something Sarah recognised as commitment as they celebrated their reconciliation in the way she'd been dreaming of since the joy first experienced only weeks before. So short a time, really, she thought dreamily when they lay quiet in each other's arms at last, yet it had seemed like the longest, bleakest period in her entire life. Suddenly she remembered something.

'Where are you going?' Alex demanded, reaching for her as she slid out of bed.

'I'm a bit of a closet romantic myself—I've got a present for you,' she said, smiling at him from the door. 'Also my dressing gown's in the other room. I can't wander round like this.'

He gave her a gleaming smile. 'I don't see why not.' Then he frowned, looking round him at the impersonal room, which was uncluttered and immaculate save for the violently untidy bed. 'Where are your things, Sarah?'

'Next door. I've been sleeping in the spare room.' Her eyes met his. 'For reasons you may possibly appreciate I couldn't sleep in this bed.'

He held out his arms. 'Come back.'

'In a minute.'

Sarah ran to her room, wrapped herself in her dressing gown and took a small box from her bedside drawer. She went back to Alex and slid into bed beside him. He held out a closed fist to her.

'Talking of romantics...' He opened his hand to display an amber earring lying on the hard palm. 'I've been carrying this round ever since that night to convince myself it really happened.'

Sarah flung her arms round his neck and kissed him passionately before handing over the box. 'Have you really?'

'If I'd thought you'd do that I'd have shown it to you ages ago. Now, what's this?' Alex took off the lid and stared at the ancient brass object inside. 'A key!' he said huskily.

'That's right. A symbolic gesture.' She smiled, pushing back her tangled hair. 'I had it ready to give to you that day. After the famous burglary. I wanted us to be together before anything else happened to either of us. But you turned me down.'

'What an idiot!' he said hoarsely, and let out a deep sigh as he held her close. 'A key. How incredible—I assume you did Blake in school too?'

Sarah nodded, smiling. 'Oh, yes, Alex Mackenzie, I did. And not just "Tyger! Tyger! burning bright" and "Jerusalem", either. Your remark that day, about the gates of paradise, struck a chord. I looked it up.'

Alex grinned. 'I was so damn proud of my exit line until I realised that, far from coming up with something brilliantly original, I was actually quoting Blake—something about "Mutual Forgiveness of each vice,/Such are the Gates of Paradise". I looked it up too.' He looked down at the small, filigreed object in his hand. 'And now you've given me the key.'

Sarah nodded, her eyes suspiciously bright. 'I knew you'd see the point.'

'You bet I do.' He caught her close and rubbed noses with her. 'I'm clever.'

'*And* modest!'

'And very, very hungry.' Alex gazed at her hopefully. 'I don't suppose you'd have any food around, darling?'

'Of course.' She smiled smugly. 'I've laid on a special dinner for just this very occasion.'

Alex hugged her tightly. 'I knew I had some reason for loving you so much. What are we having?'

Sarah slid from the bed, giggling. 'Steaks, of course. What else? Only this time without the fire brigade as unexpected guests!'

ARE YOU A FAN
OF MILLS & BOON®
MODERN ROMANCES?

If YOU are a regular United Kingdom buyer of Mills & Boon's modern Romances you might like to tell us your opinion of the books we publish to help us in publishing the books *you* like.

Mills & Boon have a Reader Panel for their Enchanted™ and Presents™ Romances. Each person on the panel receives a questionnaire every third month asking her for *her* opinion of the books she has read in the past three months. All people who send in their replies will have a chance of winning a FREE six month's of Enchanted or Presents books, sent by post—48 free in all!

If you would like to be considered for inclusion on the Panel please give us details about yourself below. All postage will be free. Younger readers are particularly welcome.

Year of birth..................................... Month ....

Age at completion of full-time education ....

Single □   Married □   Widowed □   Divorced □

Your name (print please) ....

Address...

....

.... Postcode ....

**THANK YOU! PLEASE PUT IN ENVELOPE AND POST TO
MILLS & BOON READER PANEL, FREEPOST SF195
PO BOX 152, SHEFFIELD S11 8TE**

MILLS & BOON®

Next Month's Romances

♡

Each month you can choose from a wide variety of romance novels from Mills & Boon. Below are the new titles to look out for next month from the Presents and Enchanted series.

Presents™

Enchanted™

Available from WH Smith, John Menzies, Volume One, Forbuoys, Martins, Woolworths, Tesco, Asda, Safeway and other paperback stockists.

'Happy' Greetings!

Would you like to win a year's supply of Mills & Boon® books? Well you can and they're free! Simply complete the competition below and send it to us by 31st August 1997. The first five correct entries picked after the closing date will each win a year's subscription to the Mills & Boon series of their choice. What could be easier?

ACSPPMTHYHARSI

_ _ _ _ _ _ _ _ _ _ _ _ _

TPHEEYPSARA

 _ _ _ _ _ _ _ _ _ _ _

RAHIHPYBDYTAP

_ _ _ _ _ _ _ _ _ _ _ _ _

NHMYRTSPAAPNERUY

_ _ _ _ _ _ _ _ _ _ _ _ _ _ _

DYVLTEPYAANINSEPAH

_ _ _ _ _ _ _ _ _ _ _ _ _ _ _

YAYPNAHPEREW

 _ _ _ _ _ _ _ _ _ _ _ _

DMHPYAHRYOSETPA

_ _ _ _ _ _ _ _ _ _ _ _ _ _

VRHYPNARSAEYNPIA

_ _ _ _ _ _ _ _ _ _ _ _ _ _

Please turn over for details of how to enter ☞

How to enter...

There are eight jumbled up greetings overleaf, most of which you will probably hear at some point throughout the year. Each of the greetings is a 'happy' one, i.e. the word 'happy' is somewhere within it. All you have to do is identify each greeting and write your answers in the spaces provided. Good luck!

When you have unravelled each greeting don't forget to fill in your name and address in the space provided and tick the Mills & Boon® series you would like to receive if you are a winner. Then simply pop this page into an envelope (you don't even need a stamp) and post it today. Hurry—competition ends 31st August 1997.

Mills & Boon 'Happy' Greetings Competition
FREEPOST, Croydon, Surrey, CR9 3WZ

Please tick the series you would like to receive if you are a winner

Presents™ ❑   Enchanted™ ❑   Medical Romance™ ❑
Historical Romance™ ❑   Temptation® ❑

Are you a Reader Service Subscriber?   Yes ❑   No ❑

Ms/Mrs/Miss/Mr _____
(BLOCK CAPS PLEASE)

Address _____

_____

_____ Postcode _____

(I am over 18 years of age)

One application per household. Competition open to residents of the UK and Ireland only.
You may be mailed with other offers from other reputable companies as a result of this application. If you would prefer not to receive such offers, please tick box. ❑

C7B